Tell-Tale Publishing's

4th Annual

Horror Anthology

Printed in the United States of America

TABLE OF CONTENTS

The Raven Queen

J.C. Logan

Chapter One

Black Bear's Decision, 1862

The morning sun crested the foothills to the east. It would be a warm day but the brightening sky did little to remove the chill from Caleb Mason's bones. His breath frosted the Pennsylvania air, rising into the sky before being dispersed by the gentle breeze. That breeze felt cool on his skin and raised gooseflesh on his arms.

He looked at the men and boys standing to his right and to his left. Some hung their head, others looked to the sky and whispered useless prayers. A few of them breathed so quickly they resembled a steam engine. Their fear was as palpable as the sweat which covered his forehead. These men thought they had a good idea of what was about to happen. Caleb was fairly certain only a handful of the officers knew the truth of their situation.

He had not intended to eavesdrop. The previous night he was unable to sleep. He walked the camp, past the men sleeping fitfully and the ones on guard duty. Those who were awake regarded him with pity or else averted their eyes. None spoke. At the time he was unsure if perhaps these men simply did not like him. At fourteen years he was the youngest among them. Did they doubt his nerve in battle? Maybe, but that was not it. A pall hung over the camp last night. Every man, it seemed, knew the outcome of tomorrow's battle as if they had already experienced it. Yet they did not flee. Caleb felt proud of them, proud of himself, he supposed, in some small way. Even the moments when he considered sneaking away, brief as they were, he stood fast. If tomorrow would truly be the last day for these men, it would be for him, as well. He owed it to them. He owed it to his family. And to himself.

The air was not as thick with the sense of despair as it was now, but it was present nonetheless. These men, soldiers and farmers and blacksmiths, men who had fought bravely and with honor since before Caleb joined them, were afraid. It was seeing fear in their eyes that made Caleb's heart beat a little faster.

As he walked the camp he passed by Colonel Williamson's tent. The men inside probably tried to keep their voices low but to Caleb, they may as well have been shouting. The news was not good. The Confederates had pushed their way north with surprising ease. They were camped not more than seven miles distant, and they were many. One of the officers stated the Confederates held a three-to-one advantage in both infantry and cavalry. Another advocated for retreat. Colonel Williamson scoffed and stated they would stand their ground and meet the enemy. Caleb, never before privy to an officers' meeting, hid in the shadows when they filed out of the colonel's tent. Most looked resigned to death.

Caleb did not sleep the rest of the night. He sat by a fire and counted his ammunition and powder bags. He considered writing a letter to his mother back home in Waterbury, Connecticut. But what was the point? The messengers had been dispatched earlier that evening and were unlikely to return before the battle started. So he sat at the base of a large oak and looked at the night sky and thought of his mother and sisters.

Now he looked at the men standing beside him. One in particular caught his eye. He was older than most and the only man in the regiment who did not seem to regard Caleb with open suspicion. His name was Black Bear. If Caleb could be said to have a friend among these men, it would be this strange man from somewhere out west.

Black Bear's appearance, his demeanor, his prowess in battle, all had fascinated Caleb. The boy asked endless questions whenever he found himself without duties to perform. Black Bear humored him, probably because no one else was willing to speak to him. The men of the regiment regarded him with open suspicion and even fear. As had Caleb at first.

The Indian warrior was tall and muscular. His arms and chest were covered with scars. A rather large pouch was slung over his shoulder and its contents were the source of much speculation among the men. They also kept a close watch on the two hatchets he wore tucked into his belt. In Caleb's brief time with the regiment he had never seen Black Bear so much as touch a rifle. When battle came it was upon his hatchets he relied.

But what most eyes were drawn to, what kept the men around him clutching their rifles and swords, was the object tucked into the back of Black Bear's belt. The first time Caleb had seen it, he stared at it and took a few steps back from the big man. It was an enormous bear claw. The story was that Black Bear had taken it from a very large animal that had attacked him when he was just a boy. Some of the men believed he was no more than five or six years-old when this occurred. Some said the boy was unarmed and took down the bear with sheer savagery. One thing all the stories and opinions agreed upon was that Black Bear was not to be trifled with under any circumstances. Caleb agreed.

Black Bear's expression was not one of fear, as it was with the other men around them. His eyes were narrow and focused on the tree line before them. His hands rested on the handles of his hatchets, his breathing was slow and measured. *This is a true warrior*, Caleb thought for the fifth or sixth time since he first saw Black Bear. *I wish I were as brave*.

A horn sounded in the distance. It cut through the morning air like a blade. Several men took an instinctive step back. Those who were praying ceased their prayers and clutched their rifles a bit tighter. Caleb shifted his feet and glanced in Black Bear's direction. Black Bear remained motionless as ever, his eyes fixed straight ahead.

When the Confederates came, the battle did not go as Caleb or Colonel Williamson envisioned. For one thing, the enemy's numbers were not overwhelming. They appeared made up of mostly militia with a smattering of junior officers leading the charge. Casualties were high on both sides but the Unionists held their ground. Caleb stood his ground and fired his rifle three times. Two had missed hitting anyone; the third and final shot struck a militiaman's shoulder. The impact spun the man as if by an invisible dance partner. He staggered back and was lost in the smoke and noise of the battle.

"Is that it? Did we beat them?" Caleb asked as the Confederates retreated back the way they had come.

"Perhaps," Black Bear replied.

But they had not. The morning mist and the smoke from the guns had thinned considerably and now Caleb could see movement along the tree line roughly two hundred feet from where he stood. The bulk of the Confederate regiment, in numbers even greater than the colonel's estimate, emerged from the darkness of the woods.

"Load!" Colonel Williamson shouted.

The men fidgeted at first but their commanding officer's order cut through their fear. They commenced reloading their rifles.

This time the battle went more as Caleb thought it would. The Confederates came in waves that seemed endless. The Union soldiers fell in droves, Colonel Williamson among them. Caleb did as he could but he was one boy and the enemy was relentless. As the Union line collapsed into total disarray, Black Bear took a blast of buckshot to his left shoulder. The big Indian spun from the impact and dropped the hatchet. Blood trickled down his arm. Caleb gasped. If a mighty warrior such as Black Bear could be felled...

But he did not fall. He seemed to take a moment to collect himself. Then he grabbed Caleb and ran for the top of the hill behind them.

"We're going to die," Caleb said. He was surprised by the flat tone of his voice. He was not frightened; he simply stated the inevitable.

"Cover me," Black Bear barked.

He dropped the bag slung over his shoulder and rooted through its contents. He grunted against the pain in his shoulder and seemed to teeter on the brink of unconsciousness. Caleb looked back over his shoulder. His regiment was gone. Many men lay upon the ground while the few who still lived ran in every direction. The Confederates gave chase and fired their rifles at them. Caleb licked his lips. His turn was about to come.

Black Bear pulled a small black object from his bag. Caleb did not know what it was but it was carved into a monstrous shape. Something about the idol sent fresh shivers up his spine. Black Bear whispered words that Caleb could not understand.

The boy glanced down the hill. One hundred or so Confederate soldiers charged toward the two of them, shouting and cursing. Caleb clutched his rifle to his chest. This was it.

Something very large surged past him. It took a moment for Caleb to realize it was Black Bear. The warrior hurled himself at the enemy soldiers. Covering his right hand was the giant bear claw. Caleb watched with awful fascination as the Indian crashed into the wall of gray uniforms. Some of the men screamed, several rifle shots rang out. Cutting through the chaotic noise was the scream of a mighty warrior falling before his foes.

That was when something cold and black erupted from the ground. The force of it knocked Caleb off his feet as swiftly as it knocked the air from his lungs. His rifle flew from his hands and was lost. Caleb heard the enemy soldiers gasp and shout. Several more rifles fired at once. When he looked at the enemy, he saw they no longer aimed their rifles at him. Something stood between him and them. It was a zone of darkness but something even darker moved within it, moved in the direction of the Confederate soldiers.

Then Caleb knew no more.

Chapter Two

The Sullivans, 1914

Shawn Sullivan was twelve years-old and he doubted he would see thirteen.

His life had been anything but typical until now. He had lived in Belfast with his father, mother, and younger sister, Maureen. His father's brother, Shawn's Uncle Richard, had telegrammed that America was everything he thought it would be. Jobs were plentiful and there was a lot of money to be made. Uncle Richard had lived there only two years but he already owned a house and was contemplating purchasing an automobile. "If there's that kind of money there, we have to go," Shawn's father had told his mother. And so the Sullivan family packed their bags and boarded an ocean liner for the new world.

Unfortunately, the ocean liner was the *Titanic*. Shawn, his mother and sister found their way into a lifeboat but his father was not as lucky. The last time Shawn saw him, he was standing by the rail watching his family lowered down the side of the sinking ship. Shawn remembered his father's expression. It was sad but there was a hint of something else there, as well. Shawn could not have identified what it was at the time but he figured it out eventually. *Relief*. His father, even knowing he would not make it, was relieved his family would survive.

And they had. Rescued by another ship and brought to New York City, Uncle Richard awaited them on the pier. He brought them to his house in the Bronx and there they lived for a while. One year almost to the day they arrived in New York, the family was on a train heading west.

"Pennsylvania," Uncle Richard told them. He had gotten a foreman job at one of the steel mills that paid even more than he was making in New York. And even better, he had already bought a house only one hour's walk from the factory. This was where they would live.

Shawn had been excited at the time. His excitement waned, however, when he saw the house. It sat atop a hill like the world's largest gravestone. It was painted gray, which matched the sky that day. The grounds were spacious and trees followed the property line as far as Shawn could see. It should have been beautiful. He should have been thrilled to live in a house such as this. All he felt was dread.

It started for him the night Maureen climbed into his bed. She was shaking and her cheeks were wet with tears. Shawn, groggy and not a little upset that he had been woken up, asked, "Whasamatter?" Maureen cried and hugged him tightly. With one hand she pointed to the bedroom door.

Something stood in the doorway. It was big, far too big to be Uncle Richard. It was silhouetted against the hallway electric light, which their mother kept on all night so Maureen wouldn't be afraid of the dark. It looked like a man, albeit one with long hair. And there was something wrong with his right arm. It was larger than his left and its fingers seemed to end in claws.

Any thoughts of being the brave big brother flew from Shawn's head. He screamed. Maureen covered her ears and screamed, too. Shawn looked away, holding his sister so tight neither of them could draw a deep breath. When he looked up again his mother and Uncle Richard were running into the room. The thing in the doorway was gone.

But it did not stay gone. Over the next several weeks he and Maureen saw the thing on more than a few occasions. Shawn never got a good look at it; it always seemed to stay in the shadows, or maybe it generated the darkness itself. He got the impression the man—if it was a man—wore strange-looking leggings and no shirt.

And Shawn's eyes were always drawn to the man's right arm, the one that ended in a giant, meaty paw. Its claws often gleamed in whatever meager light reached the thing.

And worse, it was not alone. The birds started showing up outside the house. He could hear them. The first time he scrounged up the courage to peek out his window. The trees that bordered the yard were full of black birds. They cawed and cackled and growled their dirges. Two times after that there were even a few who perched themselves directly outside his window. They did not fly away when Shawn looked their way. One time he threw a book at the window hard enough to chip the glass. The birds held their ground. Shawn did not try to drive them away after that.

And sometimes Shawn saw a woman. He thought it was a woman, despite being able to see no details of the figure. This one was even darker than the man-animal. Except for her eyes. They were such a bright red they nearly glowed. As scared as he was of the man and the oddly-brave black birds, the woman was much worse. Maureen saw them, too. She was just as frightened as was he, but she rarely spoke of them. She walked around the house with her doll clutched to her chest and humming to herself.

Shortly after the woman-thing made her presence known, life in the house deteriorated very quickly. Uncle Richard, to this point loving and supportive of his adopted family, became distant, and then outright hostile. He spent long hours cleaning his hunting rifle. He would take the thing apart, clean every individual piece, place it atop the fireplace mantle, then take it down ten minutes later and start again. Their mother spent much of her time in her rocking chair. First she sewed new clothes for them, but eventually she stopped sewing and simply rocked back and forth and stared out the window. Every so often she would wince and cover her ears as if she had heard a loud noise, although the house was quiet.

Then, just last week, Shawn saw his first soldier. The man's coat and trousers were as gray as the outside of the house. He carried a rifle and appeared to be hunting someone in the front yard. When he saw Shawn the soldier swung the rifle in the boy's direction. Shawn saw the muzzle flash but he heard no shot. He was also unharmed. When he opened his eyes the soldier was gone. Shawn hid in his room the rest of that day.

He tried to tell his mother about the strange people in the house only once. She did not react as he had expected. Tears filled his mother's eyes but she said nothing. She continued to stare out the window.

Now, Shawn sat on his bed, Maureen next to him. The door was closed and he had managed through great effort to slide his dresser in front of it. A great deal of noise was occurring downstairs. He heard shouts and things breaking. With every new noise Maureen buried her head a little deeper in his chest. The poor girl was sobbing and every few moments she would let out a sharp cry. Shawn held her close to him.

Footsteps coming up the stairs quite quickly. A banging on his bedroom door. "Shawn! Maureen!" It was their mother.

Shawn's first thought was to run to the door. He could probably muscle the dresser aside if he gave it everything he had. He started to move but his sister wrapped her arms around him more tightly and made him grunt. "It's mommy! I have to let her in!"

"No," Maureen sobbed. "Don't open the door, Shawn."

He tried again to free himself from her but her grip felt like that of an iron vice.

"Stay in there, children," their mother called from the other side of the door. "Don't come out no matter what you hear!"

"Mommy!" Shawn tried for the door again but he could not escape his sister's grip.

Then, silence. The sounds of crashing and breaking things from downstairs ceased suddenly. Their mother, if she remained just outside the room, had also gone quiet.

Footsteps coming up the stairs again. The pace was slow, deliberate. Each one was loud, like the banging of a huge drum. Was it Uncle Richard? No, Shawn did not think so. Whatever this was it could not be human.

Faintly, so softly Shawn could barely hear it, his mother's voice. "Please."

A loud *thud*. A shrill scream that ended abruptly. The sound of something limp and wet hitting the floor. More silence.

Maureen whimpered. "Mommy."

Shawn swallowed. His eyes darted about the room. They settled on the window. "Maureen, come on." He expected her to resist but she did not. If anything, she was a little too complacent in her move to obey him. There was no life to her movements, no purpose. She let go of her brother, accepted his hand when he offered it, and followed him to the window.

Shawn looked outside. The birds were loud tonight, louder than they had ever been. He could not see them; could, in fact, see nothing but darkness. Even the moonlight was denied them. He knew it was a good fifteen feet from his bedroom window to the ground below. Way too far but he saw no other way. He turned back to Maureen. "I'll go first. Then it's your turn, okay? I'll catch you. We're going to be okay, Maureen." Shawn opened the window. A warm August breeze washed over him and chilled the sweat that coated his face and neck. The bird sounds increased in volume until Maureen raised her hands to her ears.

Shawn had one leg out the window when his bedroom door and the heavy dresser in front of it exploded. Wood splinters pelted him and drew blood. Shawn shielded his eyes. Before he did he saw his sister had managed to throw his blanket up in front of her. It billowed with numerous impacts but Maureen appeared unharmed. Shawn turned toward the remains of his bedroom door.

The shadow woman with the red eyes stood in the doorway. Thick black smoke seemed to radiate from her. It quickly overpowered the electric light in the hall, plunging his bedroom into complete darkness.

"Children," the woman-thing said.

Someone screamed. Shawn, to his horror, realized the scream was coming from him.

Chapter Three

Mr. Bisaillon's 8th Grade Class, Now

Xavier Valsaint was feeling pretty good about himself. Not only was this the best field trip of which he had ever taken part, but he killed it when their guide at the science center asked what he must have thought were pretty tough questions. Xavier knew the answers, all of them. Okay, he guessed on one of them, and he did let Nevaeh answer one just so he wouldn't get picked on when they boarded the bus back to James Buchanan Middle School. But still, it was a good day. He especially liked how Mr. Bisaillon nodded his approval every time Xavier's hand went up. "This kid should be on *Jeopardy!*" their guide suggested after the fourth or fifth correct reply. This was answered with agreement by the teacher and grumbles from the rest of the class, especially from Kyle Reed. Xavier knew he would likely have to answer to Kyle later. The class bully was too focused on him for there to be no repercussions. But for now, he was going to be happy.

He should have texted his mother as soon as the class exited the museum. He had intended to, but as Kyle walked past he brushed Xavier with his shoulder and made the boy drop his *Avengers* backpack. Xavier was aggravated and all thoughts of calling his mom vanished. He didn't say anything to Kyle, who waited at the bus door as if daring Xavier to open his mouth. Xavier simply picked up his backpack and boarded the bus, careful not to bump into the larger boy. He took a seat next to Carlos and hoped Kyle would pick one far away. As it turned out, the class bully chose a seat at the very back of the bus, glaring another kid out of it. So for the trip home, at least, Xavier might be in the clear.

But he still hadn't called his mother. And now it was too late. The bus had left all signs of civilization behind and they were now in what his Uncle Marcus termed "the sticks." Forests thick with trees lined both sides of the two-lane road upon which the school bus travelled. Occasionally an open field would pop up on either side of the road but those were few and far between. His cell read NO SERVICE every time he tried it. That was okay. He would rather tell his mom in person and watch her expression of pride with his own eyes instead of imagining it over a text.

Carlos didn't have much to say and that was just fine. Xavier didn't feel much like talking, either. The school year was almost finished, would, in fact, be over already if they hadn't had so many snow days this year. Xavier had enjoyed those snow days, each and every one of them, but now he was paying the piper. Days off in December and January meant more school days in June. Even this didn't get him down, so pleased was he by his performance at the museum. They had nine more days to go and then the summer was his.

The bus rumbled along the country road all by itself. Now that he thought about it, Xavier couldn't remember seeing even one car since the buildings and houses gave way to trees. It made him think of the video games his older brother played. Luke always seemed to favor the games that dealt with the end of the world. He would sit on the edge of his bed and shoot zombies and blow up old cars. Whenever Xavier asked to play, it was always, "You're too young," or, if Luke was having a tough time in the game, "Get out of my face!" There were no zombies out here, and no old, rusted cars by the side of the road. Just trees. Xavier was starting to miss the city.

The bus jolted. Several kids gasped, a couple let out a short, piercing scream, most braced their arms against the seat in front of them. Xavier leaned into the aisle and looked forward. A jet of what appeared to be white smoke was blasting the windshield. The bus driver, a portly woman with her short brown hair pulled back in a tight bun atop her head, swore loudly and piloted the bus to the side of the road. Several kids laughed aloud at the woman's choice of vocabulary.

The bus came to a stop. The white smoke continued to rise from somewhere outside the front of the bus. "Radiator," Xavier heard the driver say. She opened the door and exited the bus.

Mr. Bisaillon stood and held up both hands. "Calm down, boys and girls, calm down. It's okay. There's a problem with the bus. Just stay seated and we'll all be fine."

Kids began whispering to each other. Some laughed, some looked not quite scared but certainly concerned. Xavier was one of them. He didn't know much about automotive technology, but he knew the radiator was serious business. A busted radiator meant they weren't going anywhere. Mr. Bisaillon did not appear worried. He stood at the front of the bus, alternating his gaze from the students to outside the window. Xavier would give anything to see what the bus driver was doing but he knew better than to leave his seat. So he sat and looked out the window and tried not to think about all that white smoke outside.

After several moments the bus driver came back inside. She sat in her seat and Mr. Bisaillon leaned down to speak with her. Xavier watched them intently. He couldn't hear a word they were saying but their body language confirmed his fears. There was something very wrong with the bus and they were likely not going anywhere anytime soon.

Finally, Mr. Bisaillon stood and regarded the students. "All right, listen up. I said listen up. Be quiet in the back! We have a small problem here. There's a mechanical issue with the bus. The driver is calling her dispatcher. I want everyone to remain in their seats. You can speak quietly to one another but I don't want to hear any shouting. If the noise level rises too much you'll have to sit there quietly."

Great, Xavier thought, *stuck in the middle of nowhere with Kyle Reed.* It would only be a matter of time before his nemesis got it into his head to sit behind Xavier and start the tormenting. Mr. Bisaillon and the bus driver were too occupied up front to notice when that happened. Xavier gripped his backpack a little tighter and hoped the bigger boy wouldn't decide that now was a good time for some schoolyard justice.

Mr. Bisaillon stood again and said, "If you have a cell phone please get it out and see if you have service."

"What's the matter?" Nevaeh asked.

"The matter is the radio can't get a signal out here," the bus driver grumbled without turning in her seat. She let fly a few more curse words, causing most of the kids to laugh. Mr. Bisaillon threw her a sour look but the woman seemed not to notice.

"We're stuck?" Carlos asked. His voice cracked at the end.

"We're perfectly safe," Mr. Bisaillon replied. "Just check your cells, please."

Several kids did so, Xavier included. The top left corner of his iPhone still read NO SERVICE. He looked at Mr. Bisaillon and shook his head. No one else had better luck. After several moments during which his students reported they had no signal, Mr. Bisaillon conferred again with the bus driver. Xavier wished he could hear what they were saying but he could not, even when their voices rose above a whisper.

Finally, Mr. Bisaillon stood again and said, "There was a house about a mile and a half back. I'm going to go there and see if I can use their phone. I want everyone to behave responsibly while I'm gone. Mrs. Darby is in charge. If I hear about any issues when I get back you'll be getting homework every night for the rest of the school year."

The noise level on the bus skyrocketed. Mr. Bisaillon spoke with the bus driver again. She seemed less than thrilled to be left in charge of the class. Their conversation was again animated but still Xavier couldn't hear a word. He glanced back at Kyle Reed. The boy was staring at him and smiling. His eyes conveyed what was on his mind: *As soon as Bisaillon's off this bus, you are* mine. Xavier raised his hand.

Mr. Bisaillon looked up and saw him. "Yes, Xavier?"

"Can I come?"

The question seemed to set off most of the kids on the bus. Several more hands shot into the air and many voices repeated Xavier's question. Xavier kept his hand raised. He resisted the urge to look back to see if Kyle mimicked him.

After several moments of noise and waving arms, Mr. Bisaillon quieted the bus. "I don't suppose it'll hurt," he said to Mrs. Darby.

"And less for me to deal with," she replied.

"Fewer."

"What?"

"Nevermind." Mr. Bisaillon looked at his class. "Xavier, Carlos, Nevaeh, Andy and Maya, you can come with me."

More noise and complaining from the kids who were not selected. Xavier was thrilled and he made no attempt to hide it. It was a long walk to that house but it sure beat waiting for Kyle to slide into the seat behind him and go to work. Xavier grabbed his backpack and stood.

Mr. Bisaillon raised his hands and shouted, "Okay, that's enough! Remember what I said about homework." That quieted down most of the students. Some still grumbled their complaints at being left behind but they did so now at a much lower volume. The kids chosen to go stood and started for the front of the bus, Xavier among them.

Mr. Bisaillon stopped at the door. He turned back to his students and knelt in front of them. He lowered his voice so only his chosen companions could hear him. "Leave your backpacks here. We don't know how long we'll be walking and you don't want to carry around the extra weight."

The students obediently unslung their backpacks. They were handed over to classmates they trusted. Xavier handed his to Dawn Kitney, his sometime-partner in science class projects. She took it and wished him luck. Xavier rejoined Mr. Bisaillon's small group of rescuers by the bus door.

"Yo, Mr. Bisaillon," Kyle called from his seat.

The teacher frowned and replied, "What is it, Kyle?"

"Can't I come? I don't wanna stay here. It's boring."

Several children giggled, a few laughed aloud. Mr. Bisaillon appeared less than thrilled.

"Don't say yes, don't say yes, don't say yes," Xavier whispered as he neared his teacher. It was no secret Mr. Bisaillon – indeed most of the staff at James Buchannan – had no love for Kyle Reed. He had been a troublemaker since kindergarten and his behavior had only gotten worse in the years since. Xavier was quite certain his teacher would make the boy stay behind.

"Sure, why not?" Mr. Bisaillon said. He sounded resigned.

Xavier's heart sank into his stomach. He wanted to take back his offer to accompany his teacher. But that would be even worse. Everyone in the class would know why and they were not likely to forget over the summer. He would leave middle school and enter high school with the reputation of a coward. So he said nothing. He no longer walked excitedly to the door; his feet shuffled along the floor and his head was down. Mr. Bisaillon patted him on the back but Xavier barely noticed. He prepared himself for a long walk through the middle of nowhere with his least favorite person in the world walking beside him.

The day had started out very well. Its ending was quite the opposite.

Chapter Four

The Walk, The House, The Thing in the Woods

The good news was there was still plenty of daylight left. The sun was high and their shadows walked alongside them as the small group walked back the way they had come. Xavier looked over his shoulder and saw the bus as a small yellow object on the side of the road. The white smoke had decreased in volume and intensity when the students picked for this excursion stood beside it and Mr. Bisaillon went over the rules. By the time they started walking the white smoke had reduced itself to a thin but steady stream drifting lazily into the sky. From this distance it was no longer visible. Xavier hoped against logic that Mrs. Darby would find a way to get it started and come pick them up. His enthusiasm for finding that house diminished considerably as soon as Kyle Reed was allowed to join them.

Xavier looked at everybody but him. Mr. Bisaillon walked in the lead. Every few steps he would glance over his shoulder at his fellow walkers. The girls, Nevaeh and Maya, walked behind him. They spoke quietly amongst themselves and walked as if this were the normal outcome for a field trip. Nevaeh was the taller of the two, with skin the color of alabaster. Xavier thought she was pretty if a bit arrogant in class. She could beat him in reading, but he had it all over her in science and math.

Maya was short, with long black hair that reminded Xavier of his mom's. She could also be described as pretty. Her voice was thick with an Hispanic accent but her English was perfectly understandable. Xavier envied her a little for her bilingual ability. He often wished he could speak more than one language.

Andy was the blondest kid Xavier had ever seen. He didn't spend a lot of time around him but he knew Andy was a big Phillies fan. He often went into the city to watch his favorite team play. The only time Andy resented a Phillies loss was when it came against the Mets. On those days Andy was nearly inconsolable. Xavier was more of a basketball man himself - a huge fan of LeBron, naturally - so the two had little in common. He liked Andy enough but they rarely spoke or interacted in class, and never outside of it. In fact, Xavier realized, this was the first time the two of them were in close proximity without the benefit of being in a classroom.

Carlos walked beside Xavier. He didn't say much, which was his norm. Xavier could have used a bit of conversation and Carlos was his best bet. But the short kid with his short brown hair and short brown socks did not offer any.

Kyle was, obviously, out of the question.

That left only Mr. Bisaillon. Xavier already had enough problems with Kyle Reed. He didn't need a reputation as a teacher's pet any more than he needed that of a coward. And so Xavier walked in silence.

He checked the time on his phone. *At least that works*, he thought. It was 3:17 in the afternoon. Yes, plenty of daylight left. They just had to get to this house and talk the people there into letting them use their phone. It was likely to be quite some time before anyone could come and pick them up and bring them home. Xavier did some fast calculations and figured he wouldn't get there until well after 8, and that was if he was lucky. He was not feeling particularly lucky at the moment.

A small rock skidded past Xavier's feet. It was the third such rock he'd seen since they left the bus. As with the other two he turned and saw Kyle smiling at him. This was getting on Xavier's nerves. He doubted he could take Kyle in a fight, was almost certain he could not, but each time the other boy kicked a rock at him, Xavier felt a burning sensation behind his eyes. If they didn't find this house soon there was going to be trouble.

The group continued on, Mr. Bisaillon in the lead. They did not see a single car or truck driving in either direction. If not for the power lines just off the side of the road they could have travelled back in time 100 years. It was also quiet, *too* quiet for Xavier. He was used to the sounds of traffic and people having loud conversations up and down his street. Of sirens, either distant or near, wailing through his neighborhood. He simply wasn't used to this kind of silence.

The one upside to his current location was the smell of the air. It was cleaner out here. He had become accustomed to the smell of car exhaust and garbage, and even body odor, the latter mostly at school. Out here everything smelled different. It was pine and grass and animals and wildflowers. As unnerving as it was, he thought he could get used to it pretty easily.

The trees on the right side of the road revealed a gap in their line. What looked to be a very narrow dirt road wound its way into a dense patch of trees and foliage. The group stopped there.

"I think this is it," Mr. Bisaillon announced.

"This is what?" Andy asked.

Mr. Bisaillon pointed to the dirt road. "This is the driveway to that house. I think." The teacher stood on his toes and craned his neck. "Can't see over the trees." He regarded his students. "Maya, help me out."

"How?" the girl asked.

Mr. Bisaillon dropped to one knee. "Climb on my back, then stand up on my shoulders. I'll lift you up. See if you can spot the house."

Maya did as he asked. Her legs wobbled a bit when Mr. Bisaillon stood. "Don't worry, I won't let you fall," he assured her.

The girl looked in the direction of the dirt road. Xavier saw her squint against the sunlight. She even brought up one hand to shield her eyes and looked like a soldier saluting a giant officer. Finally she said, "I see it! Mr. Bisaillon, I see a house! It's way up at the top of a hill!"

"Good job," Mr. Bisaillon replied. He lowered the girl to the ground. "Okay, follow me." He led the way off the main road and onto the dirt driveway.

The sun vanished almost as soon as they left the pavement. The trees on either side of the driveway provided an effective canopy that threw them all into near-darkness. The warm, pleasant breeze that had followed them since they left the bus disappeared at the same time. Sounds reached their ears, coming from the woods on either side. Xavier stopped and looked each time he heard something but he could see nothing. Beyond the perimeter of trees all was darkness. A sudden chill ran down his spine. The small hairs on his arms stood up and stayed that way.

An animal that must have been much larger than the squirrels he saw in his own back yard rustled in the darkness beyond his vision. Xavier had no wish to see what it was; he looked anyway. Something moved, something big, perhaps as big as he. It raced between two large, thick trees and crouched. Xavier realized he was wrong; whatever it was it was much larger than he, larger by far even than Mr. Bisaillon. His eyes went wide. He stuttered and pointed.

"What's your problem, Valsaint? Scared of the dark?"

It was Kyle. Of course it was. He had come up behind Xavier when the smaller boy's attention had been glued to the woods. Xavier looked at him, the dread he usually felt when dealing with Kyle temporarily forgotten.

"There's something in there," Xavier said. His mouth and throat felt bone dry.

"Maybe it's your mom," Kyle replied. He shoved Xavier forward with both hands.

Xavier stumbled but managed to keep his feet under him. He never took his eyes from the woods, but whatever he saw had vanished back into the darkness.

"Keep moving, moron," Kyle said, and shoved him forward again.

Xavier started moving. Every few steps he looked into the woods again but he saw nothing. Nor did he hear anything. Whatever it was must have moved on. He didn't know why, but he felt relief at the thing's departure. As if he had narrowly escaped something hideous. He caught up to the rest of the group and they continued to follow the winding driveway.

The distinctive caw of birds reached their ears. Xavier craned his neck toward the treetops. There was not much to see but he could hear the sound of their wings. As the seven refugees from James Buchanan Middle School continued their advance up the driveway the sound became louder, more intense. "There must be a thousand birds in those trees," Xavier remarked to no one in particular.

"I don't like birds," Nevaeh announced. She cast nervous eyes at the treetops.

"Hello, Alfred Hitchcock," Mr. Bisaillon commented. When he glanced at his students and saw only blank stares he sighed. "Classical reference. Google it when we get back to civilization."

They reached a clearing in the woods and suddenly the sun was in their eyes again. The glare was intense after the darkness of the last few minutes. Xavier shielded his eyes from the sun and found himself at the bottom of a large, steep hill. At the top sat a house.

It was the largest house Xavier had ever seen. It reminded him of the photos in his history books of old English manors. He wondered if perhaps it was even larger than his school. The middle section alone looked as if it could fit every house on his street within its walls. The two end sections were nearly as large and were rounded like grain silos. He counted three levels of windows plus another, smaller set at the top of the structure. A very large deck ran the width of the front of the house and disappeared around the sides.

The grounds – this could not be called a lawn – sprawled as far as he could see. The grass was neatly manicured and flower beds dotted the border of the driveway leading to the mansion. Xavier whistled through his teeth.

"There we are," Mr. Bisaillon announced. He continued to follow the driveway up the hill. If the teacher was impressed by the spectacle he kept it to himself.

Xavier's classmates, too, marveled at the sheer size of the house. Even Kyle seemed to have forgotten about him, at least for the moment. The students stood and gazed at the mansion on the hill while their teacher made his way toward it.

After a few more moments the six children followed Mr. Bisaillon. The driveway was not notably steep however Xavier felt his legs beginning to ache. Each step he took his body weight seemed to increase. He ran a hand across his forehead and it came away wet. He wiped his hand on his pants and hoped no one noticed. The girls seemed to be having a hard time, too. They had stopped talking and giggling and were now starting to breathe heavy. A look at Andy and Carlos told him they, too, were feeling the effects of their exertion. Xavier did not bother to see if Kyle was likewise getting winded.

It seemed to take hours but the group finally crested the hill and stood at the top of the dirt driveway. The house loomed in front of them, blotting out the sun. The wind kicked up and ruffled Xavier's shirt. He closed his eyes and spread his arms and let the breeze cool his skin. It felt good, great, in fact. When he opened his eyes he saw his classmates mimicking him.

All except Kyle, of course. He simply stood with his withering gaze fixed upon Xavier. His eyes said, *Okay, I'm already over this house. Time to get back to our regularly scheduled bullying.*

"You guys stay here. I'll see if they'll let us use their phone." Mr. Bisaillon waited for his students to nod their understanding and then he mounted the steps that led to the front door. He knocked, waited. No one came to the door. He knocked again. After a few more attempts he turned back to his students. "Doesn't look like they're home."

"Maybe they're in the back," Andy offered. "I bet they couldn't hear you because they're in the back yard."

"We can give it a shot," Mr. Bisaillon replied. "You guys stay here in case someone does come to the door. Andy, come with me."

The teacher and the blonde boy walked around the side of the house.

No more than a moment after their departure, the front door creaked open.

Chapter Five

Inside the House, The Soldiers

Xavier's eyes were drawn immediately to the large double doors that were the entrance to the house. Both swung open slowly and with a loud creak. The sound alone caused Xavier's heart to beat a little faster. He, along with his classmates, waited to see who would emerge from the darkness of the house.

No one did. The doors remained open and the entryway remained empty.

"Okay, that's weird," Carlos said.

Maya turned in the direction where Mr. Bisaillon had vanished. "Mr. Bisaillon! The door's open but there ain't nobody there!"

Mr. Bisaillon did not reappear from the side of the house. Maya shouted to him again. The five students from James Buchannan Middle School remained alone.

"Don't be wussies!" Kyle exclaimed. He grabbed Xavier and Carlos by their shirts and dragged both boys up the steps. When they stood in front of the doors Kyle turned his attention to the two girls. "Get up here and stop acting like babies."

Nevaeh and Maya exchanged nervous glances.

"Yo! Anybody home?" Kyle shouted into the darkness beyond the front doors. After a moment he turned back toward the two girls. "See? Nobody there. Now get up here and let's go find a phone. I'd like to get home before the summer ends!"

The girls were clearly reluctant but they mounted the steps together. They stood behind Xavier and Carlos.

"Well? Get in there!"

Kyle shoved the two boys across the threshold. He grabbed Nevaeh's arm and prodded her forward. Maya went along. Then Kyle followed them through.

The foyer was cavernous. The vaulted ceiling was at least twenty feet above their heads. A very large light fixture – an honest-to-gosh chandelier – hung from it. Two wide staircases ascended from the foyer and met at the top of the second floor. Several hallways branched away in multiple directions. The floor was hard wood and so polished Xavier could see his reflection in its surface. Several small writing tables and a few luxurious chairs dotted the foyer.

Something about the room made Xavier uneasy. He had no idea what it could be. Nothing seemed out of place, there were no signs of obvious threat. Still the hair on his arms stood and his brow was coated with sweat.

A very large and elegant living room stood to the left of the foyer. Paintings that would not have looked out of place in the Louvre decorated the walls. End tables and coffee tables competed with large chairs and sofas. A giant stone fireplace dominated one wall. A small pile of chopped wood sat next to it. The room could have accommodated every kid in the class with enough space for the kids in Ms. Porcaro's classroom next door.

"We shouldn't be in here," Xavier whispered.

"What?" Carlos asked.

Xavier cleared his throat. "I said we shouldn't be in here. Isn't this burglary or something? We could get in trouble." That was true to the best of Xavier's knowledge but it was not the real reason he wanted to leave. It wasn't even in the top five.

Kyle barked a short, loud laugh. "You're such a wuss, Valsaint. Go find a phone, loser."

"We'll go with you," Nevaeh declared. "Me and Maya."

"Me, too," Carlos tried.

"Not even close," Kyle told him. "You're sticking with me. You three morons go that way, me and this moron will go this way."

Xavier could think of nothing else to say. Of course he wanted Carlos with him but Kyle had handed down his decree and that was that. All things considered Xavier felt fortunate; at least he had Nevaeh and Maya with him instead of looking for a phone by himself, or worse, looking with Kyle. As the group parted Xavier wondered what they would say if the owners of the house showed up. Hopefully Mr. Bisaillon would hear them coming up the driveway and explain their situation. It was a well-know, if stupid, fact of life that adults tended to listen to other adults before children. He certainly didn't relish the idea of having to explain to complete strangers what he and his classmates were doing in their home.

He walked down the hall chosen by Kyle, the two girls behind him. His companions said nothing but he could hear their shuffling footsteps and quick breathing. They were scared. Xavier couldn't blame them. *He* was scared, too. If the owners showed up now they could very easily call the cops. The last thing Xavier needed was to have to call his mom from jail. Nevertheless he decided he couldn't show his fear in front of the others. Not here, not now.

The hall was long and dark. There was muted light at the end where it opened into a room. Xavier emerged from the hall into a kitchen larger than any room in his house. The floor was white linoleum and spotless. The table was circular and surrounded by twelve wooden chairs. A narrow white door stood to the side of the stove. Xavier figured it led to a pantry; his grandmother's house had a similar door and that's where she kept most of her dry foods and cans of soup. The appliances appeared old but they, too, were very clean. Colorful plastic letter magnets adorned the fridge.

Some had been arranged into a message. OUR N W HOM , it said. "Looks like they lost all the *E*s," Maya remarked.

The phone was mounted to the wall beside the refrigerator. Xavier walked to it.

"They still have a landline," Maya commented.

"Well, duh," Nevaeh replied. "No phone signal out here, remember?"

"Oh, right."

Xavier removed the handset from the cradle and placed it against his ear. He heard no dial tone. He hung up and tried again. "It doesn't work," he told the girls.

"Great," Nevaeh said. "Now what?"

As Xavier hung up the phone he caught movement out of the corner of his eye. He turned in the direction of an open doorway that led from the kitchen into another part of the house. Something had moved from the doorway, something that might have been there the whole time. Xavier gasped. The girls turned quickly toward the doorway.

"What? What is it?" Maya asked.

"There…There was someone standing there."

"Who?" This time it was Nevaeh's turn to ask.

Xavier craned his neck but he could not see into the hallway beyond the door. His first thought was to walk over and see if whoever-it-was was still there. But his legs refused to work. He stood by the phone as if his feet had grown roots into the floor.

Nevaeh's eyes took on a defiant glare. "Don't try to scare us, Xavier," she declared. The girl walked to the doorway and looked beyond. She stood there for a moment before turning her eyes to Xavier. "There's no one there. No. One. You're a jerk for trying to scare us. I'm gonna tell Mr. Bisaillon."

Xavier felt his ability to move return. He approached the doorway slowly, still craning his neck. Nevaeh was correct; the hall beyond was empty. It stretched quite a way and he counted no fewer than six doors along the walls. "I know I saw something. I thought it was a kid but I didn't get a good enough look."

"Whatever," Nevaeh announced. "Let's go find Mr. Bisaillon." She marched back the way they had come, Maya walking in step behind her.

Xavier remained in the kitchen. His eyes travelled to the large bay window that took up most of one wall. Maybe whoever he saw had gone outside. Xavier approached the window. Beyond the glass stretched the back yard of the property. Like the front the lawn was neatly mowed, the various flower gardens and trees trimmed. It sloped down toward what Xavier assumed to be more woods.

Mr. Bisaillon and Andy were back there. He saw his teacher fiddling with his cell phone. After a few moments he shook his head at Andy. The blonde boy appeared irritated. Xavier could not hear their conversation but he could guess what was going on.

Something beyond the two in the back yard caught Xavier's attention. Something moved near the downward slope of the well-manicured grounds. Xavier squinted against the glare thrown by the window glass. Someone was walking up the hill in the direction of the house. *Finally*, Xavier thought. *The owner must have been down the hill and we didn't see him.*

He was about to follow the girls back to the foyer when he saw the man walking up the hill was not alone. A second man appeared, then a third. In a few seconds there were dozens of them. Nor were they walking. Xavier searched for the right word. After a moment it came to him. These men were *marching*. They moved in lockstep with one another like the clone troopers in the *Star Wars* movies. To reinforce the image these men wore uniforms. Some were blue, others, gray, but they were pretty close in design. Each man carried what appeared to be a rifle, the long stock held against their shoulder.

Mr. Bisaillon and Andy turned and saw the soldiers marching in their direction. Andy retreated a few steps. Mr. Bisaillon seemed uncertain of what to do. He shouted something at them but the soldiers seemed not to reply. They never broke stride.

Andy grabbed at his teacher's arm and tried to pull him back. Mr. Bisaillon seemed unable to take his eyes from these new arrivals.

The soldiers swung their rifles up and pointed them in the direction of the pair in front of them. Xavier gasped.

Mr. Bisaillon grabbed Andy's hand and bolted for the front of the house.

Xavier ran, too. He reached the foyer to find the girls standing by the front door.

Maya was fighting to maintain control but it seemed obvious she was scared and trying not to cry. Nevaeh's voice held a measure of alarm when she announced, "The door's locked! It won't open!"

Carlos and Kyle appeared atop the landing where the twin staircases met and looked down at them. "What's the matter?" Carlos asked. The expression on the faces of the girls seemed to unnerve him. He sounded scared, too.

"We're locked in!" Nevaeh told him.

"Let me try," Xavier offered. Nevaeh got out of his way.

Before Xavier could try his luck Kyle descended the stairs and shouldered his way to the door. "Back up, all of ya," he ordered. The other kids did as they were told. Kyle pulled on the door handle. It made an unpleasant squeak but it did not open. Kyle stood back, regarded the door.

"We can't be trapped in here!" Maya exclaimed.

"Shut up," Kyle told her.

He tried again. The squeak repeated itself, more loudly this time. Xavier saw the door quiver in its frame. Kyle must have seen it, too. He pulled with what looked to be all his strength. The door flew open. Kyle, off-balance, flew back and crashed into one of the small writing tables. He grunted with pain.

Nevaeh and Maya were through the door in an instant, but both girls stopped in their tracks after making it only a few steps onto the deck. They screamed in unison. Xavier raced out after them.

The soldiers he had seen out back had moved to the front of the house. They marched in formation toward the front deck.

"Get inside! Get inside!"

The shout had come from the side of the house, very close. Xavier saw Mr. Bisaillon and Andy running at full speed for the front deck. Behind them came the soldiers he had seen from the kitchen window. *Now there are* two *groups*, Xavier thought, panicked.

He grabbed Nevaeh and Maya and shoved them through the front door. Xavier lost his balance and fell. The hard wood of the deck bruised his knee and made him gasp. Still he was on his feet a second later and limping for the front door. He threw himself inside the house and turned his head in the direction of the door.

Mr. Bisaillon and Andy neared the steps. Some of the soldiers in the front yard beat them to it. Xavier watched his teacher and his classmate disappear into a wall of blue and gray uniforms. He lost sight of them, although from the actions and body language of the soldiers it seemed a fight was happening. The mass of blue and gray seemed to push itself farther from the front deck, carrying both teacher and student with it.

It was instinct, not conscious thought, that moved Xavier in their direction. They needed help. He did not get far.

The trees that bordered the property exploded in an enormous black cloud. Its shape was inconsistent, with patches of daylight shining through some areas and nothing but black in others. It took Xavier a full five seconds to realize what he was looking at. Birds. Thousands of them, maybe tens of thousands. They were flying directly at the house.

The front door slammed itself closed with so much force the wood frame cracked. Xavier reeled back, his feet unable to stop his backward tumble. He landed on Kyle, who swore but seemed incapable of freeing himself from the sudden weight lying atop him.

Xavier rolled free of the other boy. That was going to cost him for sure. Kyle wouldn't care if Xavier meant to flatten him or not. He had done the deed, and he did it in front of everyone. Kyle's revenge would not be pleasant.

Xavier started to rise. A wave of nausea washed over him and dropped him to his knees again. He felt the bile rise in his throat but somehow he stopped himself from vomiting. The world seemed to shimmer around him as if he were in the middle of a heat mirage. Everything blurred and rippled and Xavier closed his eyes tight against the visual assault. The floor trembled beneath him. The hardwood felt strange and unusual. His stomach dropped into his feet; the sensation reminded him of riding the rollercoaster at the summer carnival in Wilkes-Barre. He might have whimpered and he might have produced no sound at all. His senses overwhelmed, he could do nothing but wait for the world to return to normal.

A few moments later it did. When it passed he wiped his eyes and looked again at the front door.

It had changed. In point of fact, the entire foyer had changed. The hardwood floor, so shiny he had seen his own reflection in its surface, was old and faded and pitted with cracks and small holes. The double front doors had likewise lost their luster. They were in the same shape as the floor.

Xavier's gaze moved about the foyer. The ornate staircases looked in danger of collapse. The railings were gone, the steps rotted. The chandelier lay in the middle of the foyer like a dead monster, its elegant crystal shattered into thousands of pieces. The writing tables had disintegrated into heaps of brittle, aged wood.

The living room had fared no better. The paintings were faded and some hung at odd angles. The tables and furniture had collapsed into unrecognizable heaps of rotting garbage. Some of the stones from the fireplace had fallen out and lay on the floor. The chopped wood that would have fueled the fireplace on a cold Pennsylvania night had long since decayed into pulp.

His classmates gazed in horror at the state of the foyer. Whatever hit Xavier had hit them, as well. Carlos and the girls were rising to their knees. Kyle still lay curled into a ball near the remains of one of the writing tables. His body shook and it sounded to Xavier as if the bigger boy might be crying.

Carlos, his voice a hoarse croak, was the only one who spoke. "Oh, boy."

Chapter Six

Surrounded

Xavier's knee barked at him when he tried to stand. He grimaced and rubbed the sore spot. He watched Carlos regain his feet and help the girls stand. Nevaeh recovered quickly from whatever produced that wave of nausea and she moved toward the front doors. For an awful moment Xavier thought she might actually open them. The girl instead peeked through the now-cracked glass that bordered the doors. She gasped.

"Mr. Bisaillon and Andy!" she shouted.

Xavier finally got to his feet and limped to her. He looked through the glass.

The soldiers stood in an organized line, their weapons resting against their shoulders. Mr. Bisaillon was on his hands and knees, clearly struggling to rise. His tie was gone and his shirt torn. Blood seeped slowly from his nose. Andy, looking in better shape than his teacher and kneeling next to him, helped Mr. Bisaillon to his knees. Both placed their hands behind their head after one of the soldiers barked something at them.

So focused was he on what was happening to his teacher and classmate, it took Xavier a few moments to note the changes that had taken place outside the house.

The deck was rotted and worn. Several boards were missing and large holes dotted its once-pristine appearance. The front yard had also changed. The grass was no longer neatly cut. In fact, it looked as if it had not seen a lawn mower since before Xavier was born. The grass was tall and full of weeds. The soldiers stood in formation, their rifles resting on their shoulders. A few of them, most likely officers, paced back and forth among the lines, barking orders Xavier could not hear. Four of them stood guard next to Andy and Mr. Bisaillon.

"They're gonna kill em!" Nevaeh exclaimed.

"Please, no!" Maya screamed. She began to cry.

The soldiers made no move to harm their teacher or their classmate. They stood in their formation and neither moved nor spoke.

"Hang on," Xavier told them. "They're not doing anything, just standing there."

Carlos and Maya joined them. The four kids jostled one another for a look outside.

"They're gonna come in here," Carlos said to no one in particular.

"What do we do then? Maya asked.

"We can't possibly stop them." Xavier did not realize he had spoken aloud until he noticed the other kids staring at him in varying degrees of fear. He shrugged. What else could he say?

"We can get out the back," Carlos suggested. "If all these guys are out front there's no one in the back yard." He started back toward the kitchen. The girls followed.

"Hang on," Xavier told them. When they paused he continued, "Are we not gonna talk about what just happened? Look at this house."

His three classmates did indeed look, but only a momentary, cursory glance. None seemed to want to take it all in. Or perhaps they were incapable of doing so. Xavier was as reluctant as they but this seemed to be their reality now.

"I'm heading for the back," Carlos informed him. "You coming?"

The girls nodded their agreement and the three of them disappeared quickly down the hallway which led to the kitchen.

Xavier was about to join them when he saw Kyle getting to his feet.

"You okay?"

Kyle wiped his nose and sniffled. For a half-second he was no longer the bully. He looked small and scared and vulnerable. Then his eyes hardened and his hands balled into fists. "Shut up, idiot."

Xavier shook his head. *Well, that didn't last long.* With a final look around the foyer and the living room he headed for the kitchen. He heard Kyle fall into step behind him.

The change that had overtaken the whole front of the house had also transformed the kitchen. The linoleum was cracked and worn. The refrigerator lay on the floor much like the chandelier in the foyer. The letter magnets were scattered about and covered with dust. The cabinet doors, the ones that remained, hung from rusted hinges. The shelves inside were barren. The old phone was gone; its cord lay on the floor like a dead snake. The large table still stood in the middle of the room but it swayed a bit when Xavier bumped it on his way past.

The door Xavier assumed lead to the pantry was still in place. Its paint had faded somewhat but it seemed mostly unaffected by what had happened.

Carlos, Nevaeh and Maya stood by the windows. Their body language told Xavier what he would see even before he joined them.

There were more soldiers standing in the tall grass of the back yard. They stood and stared at the four young people at the windows.

Carlos swallowed loudly. "There's a lot more of those guys than I thought."

"So we're surrounded?" Maya's voice was high-pitched. She was close to panic, if she wasn't there already.

Xavier's eyes were drawn to the blue sky above. The birds moved in tight formation, forming a black circle that orbited above the house and the grounds. Even from inside the ruined kitchen he could hear their caws and squawks. He turned away from the door.

Xavier pulled out his cell phone again. Before he hit the power button he prayed for a few bars, or even one. One might be enough.

He exhaled loudly when he saw the same NO SERVICE message that had greeted him since the school bus broke down.

Nevaeh looked at the phone. "Wait a minute," she said. "Upstairs! We might be able to get a signal upstairs!"

"Damn, you're a moron." Kyle stood behind them. His eyes moved from the window to Nevaeh.

"Think about it," Nevaeh continued, ignoring Kyle completely. "This place is huge. The top floor is really high up. It might work."

"It's worth a shot," Xavier agreed.

Kyle shook his head. "The basement's a better idea."

Nevaeh placed her hands on her hips. "By what stretch of the imagination is the basement a better idea? You think we'll get reception down there? Now who's the moron?"

Kyle's eyes flared. He took an angry step toward Nevaeh. Xavier thought he might actually hit the girl. And he may have, had Carlos not gotten between them. It took Xavier only a moment to join the other boy. Kyle stopped in his tracks. His whole body quivered. Xavier thought at first Kyle was angry enough to take all three of them, four if Maya came to her friend's defense. But it was not anger he saw in the bigger boy's eyes. And the quivering was not of rage. Kyle was scared. That simple realization chilled Xavier. Kyle was the toughest kid in the entire school. If *he* was this scared...

"Let's just hear him out," Xavier offered. He looked closely at Kyle. He still didn't know if the bigger boy would swing on them or not. Xavier braced himself and said, "What about the basement?"

Kyle continued to glare at his classmates but Xavier's offer seemed to placate him, if only marginally. After another moment he licked his lips and said, "This old place was probably built a hundred years ago, maybe two hundred. There might be a tunnel in the basement."

Carlos sighed and rolled his eyes.

"Where'd you get that idea?" Maya asked. She now stood next to Nevaeh.

"In history class, idiot! Remember when Miss DiBella told us about the Underground Railroad? She said some houses had escape tunnels for slaves." His eyes moved rapidly across the faces of his classmates as if he were searching for the least sign of agreement. "Don't you get it? This could be one of those!"

"That's pretty thin," Carlos admitted.

"Like Valsaint said, it's worth a shot!" Kyle exclaimed. Some of the fear had left his voice. It was replaced by the usual anger and contempt Kyle Reed usually showed everyone around him.

Nevaeh sidestepped Carlos and Xavier and stood in front of Kyle. "Then you go down there and the rest of us will go upstairs and see if we can get a signal."

"Hold up," Xavier told them. He agreed with Carlos. What Kyle was suggesting was ridiculous. He did not for one moment think there was a tunnel in the basement, assuming the house even had a basement. But if Kyle turned out to be correct Xavier had no doubt the boy would follow that tunnel and leave the rest of them behind. The thought of Kyle Reed emerging into the sunlight a few miles beyond the house and those soldiers while Xavier and the others were still trapped inside...

"Okay, Kyle, go find the basement. Carlos, go with him. I'll try upstairs with Maya and Nevaeh."

Kyle seemed at least somewhat placated. He licked his lips again and nodded.

"I'm not going down into the basement," Carlos argued.

"Scared, Medina? I always knew you were a wuss," Kyle sneered. He seemed to have regained much of his usual bravado.

"Hey, I ain't no wuss," Carlos exclaimed. He was angry, that much was clear. He took a step toward Kyle.

"Oh, come on! Are we really gonna fight now? With all those guys outside? Shouldn't we be trying to get out of here and get some help for Mr. Bisaillon and Andy?"

"Xavier's right," Maya said. She looked out the window again before turning back to the others. "I don't think those guys are gonna wait all day. Sooner or later they're gonna come in here. We need to get out before then."

"Why does it have to be me?" Carlos asked.

"Fine, I'll go," Nevaeh told them. "I don't care. But Maya's right. We need to get a move on."

"You two look for the basement, the rest of us will head upstairs." Xavier spoke in his calmest tone of voice. "Deal?"

"Fine," Kyle agreed. "Meet back in the foyer in about ten minutes. Let's go, Nevaeh."

Nevaeh hugged Maya and followed Kyle out of the kitchen. Maya watched her friend leave.

"Let's head up," Xavier said. "The sooner we get out of here the better."

The three friends headed in the direction of the foyer.

Chapter Seven

The Basement, The Man-Thing and The Woman

There were several doors along each side of the hall. The first led into a study. Ancient bookshelves held equally ancient books. They looked as if they would crumble to dust if Kyle so much as got close to them. The second opened into a playroom of some kind. Old toys made of wood and metal and some very decrepit armchairs filled the room. Kyle could picture long-dead adults sitting in those chairs watching equally-long-dead children playing with those toys. He shrugged. Whatever. The third door led to a bathroom. Kyle did not even step inside, although he toyed with the idea of shoving Nevaeh in there and holding the door closed. While the thought of that made him smile he knew the girl would scream her head off and he simply didn't want to hear it.

"Did anyone try that door in the kitchen?" Nevaeh asked.

Kyle stopped. Had they? No, he was pretty sure they had not. He felt stupid—not for the first time—and he doubled back for the kitchen. He just knew Nevaeh was behind him trying not to laugh at his obvious stupidity. Kyle resisted the urge to turn on the girl and swing with everything he had.

When they reached the narrow door in the kitchen Kyle tried the handle. It turned easily enough and he swung the door open. A wood staircase led down into absolute darkness. Kyle felt along either side of the door. He found the light switch and flicked it several times but the bulb was out. Or missing.

"Great," Kyle said. "Get out your phone so we can see where we're going."

Nevaeh did as he said. She held her phone out in front of her. Its meager light illuminated a few of the steps that had been cloaked in darkness but nothing beyond.

"Head down."

Nevaeh turned to Kyle. "*You* head down. I'm not going first."

"You have the phone, genius."

Nevaeh shoved her phone at Kyle.

He sneered and took it. "Even Medina would have been better," he shot as he edged past her. The step creaked under his weight but not loudly. He took another tentative step, Nevaeh's phone held out in front of him like a shield. "Let's go."

Nevaeh waited until Kyle had descended several steps before she followed him. The steps seemed solid enough. He felt the girl place one hand on his shoulder.

The last step creaked very loudly. The sound was like a rifle shot in the darkness. Nevaeh gasped but stopped herself short of a full scale scream. Her fingernails drove into Kyle's shoulders and he hissed and turned on her.

"Sorry," she offered.

Kyle muttered "Watch it!" under his breath.

He waved her phone in a slow arc in front of him. The basement was full of large, dark shapes. The light from the girls' phone was simply not bright enough to make out anything.

"Can you see anything? Because I can't."

"Not much," Kyle admitted. "Lots of stuff down here. Can't really tell what it is. Let's try this way."

They advanced slowly into the basement. The floor felt like dirt beneath Kyle's sneakers. Although he could not see much of anything he got the impression the room was enormous, maybe the size of the gym back at school. And it smelled. He could not identify what it smelled like but it was not a pleasant odor. Mildew, maybe, or simply age. Kyle wondered how long it had been since anyone had been down here.

"Is it me or is it really cold down here?"

"Would you shut up?" Kyle hissed. But she was right. He had already repressed one shiver and he could feel more on the way. The basement was cold and getting colder the farther in they ventured.

Large shapes loomed at the edges of the phone's light. Furniture, probably. They glimpsed something covered with a sheet. An old dresser, perhaps. His grandmother had very old and very large dressers in her house. What had she called them? It was a funny-sounding name but he could not remember at the moment.

"I don't like it down here," Nevaeh announced. "It smells bad."

"So does your mom. Now be quiet."

He half-expected her to get mad and stomp back up the stairs, probably throwing a few choice words in his direction as she went. But she remained behind him, her hands on his shoulders, and said nothing.

They came upon an ancient piano. Kyle tapped a few of the keys. The notes sounded sickly and died in the stale air. He took some pleasure when Nevaeh jumped at the sounds.

"Kyle, please, let's just see if there's a tunnel so we can get out of here."

There was fear in her voice. On a normal day he would find that to be very satisfying. Then again, on a normal day, they wouldn't be in the basement of an old house that looked new when they first saw it, and their teacher wouldn't be outside surrounded by creepy-looking idiots dressed in old Army uniforms. And anyway, Nevaeh was right. They did need to find a way out. He moved away from the piano.

Kyle noticed for the first time his breath was frosting the air. He could see it in the light from Nevaeh's phone. *This is definitely not right. Why is it so damned cold down here?* He pushed the question away. He didn't care. What he did care about was finding a way out of this dump.

There were more large objects in front of them. Kyle moved past these slowly, shining the phone's light in front of him. In a few moments they reached the foundation wall. Several old and broken chairs were piled in a heap between them and the wall. He moved the light this way and that but he succeeded only in throwing shadows around. He could not tell if there was anything on the other side of the chairs other than a rock wall. No tunnel there.

"Okay, let's try over there." He started to move to his right, Nevaeh still behind him, still digging her fingernails into his shoulders.

Something growled in the darkness.

Nevaeh shrieked. Kyle winced at the pain in his ears. The girl bolted away. Kyle backed up. The phone's light revealed nothing in front of him but he had heard the growl, plain as day. He jumped a little when he heard Nevaeh all but fly up the stairs. He turned and headed in that direction.

He found the staircase easily enough. The bottom step creaked loudly again under his weight. At the top he could see the cellar door slowly swinging closed. Kyle bolted up the stairs.

One of them gave way under his feet. For a split-second he was sure the entire thing would collapse and he would be back down in the basement, alone with whatever it was that growled at them. His hands, however, had other ideas. They grasped the old railing and kept him from falling. It took a few seconds but he managed to free his foot from the splintered wood of the broken step.

At the top he could see only a sliver of light where the door was about to close. He moved as fast as he could. The door closed just as he reached it. He fumbled for the knob and turned it. The door did not budge. He pushed again. Nothing. Had Nevaeh locked him inside? If that was the case she would soon be exploring entirely new realms of pain when he got out. Girl or not, no one was going to get away with locking him down here.

The bottom step creaked.

Kyle's heart nearly stopped. His hands went numb and he dropped Nevaeh's phone. It bounced on one of the steps and then fell through. It must have broken when it hit the floor because its light vanished and plunged Kyle into complete darkness.

Whatever had reached the bottom step was coming his way. He could hear it getting closer, could hear the other steps groan beneath its weight.

Kyle turned and threw all his weight against the door. It rattled in its frame but did not open. He felt dust drifting down around him. He beat his numb fists against the door. "Let me out! Let me out! Help!"

He felt something warm on the back of his neck. It was the thing's breath. Kyle froze. All thoughts of retribution against Nevaeh flew from his mind. He likewise forgot all about his classmates searching the upper floors and about Mr. Bisaillon and Andy. In fact, he forgot about everything.

His legs felt as if they were made of rubber. He swayed and nearly fell over. Something big and strong caught him and kept him from tumbling down the stairs. Something that felt like an animal's paw, impossibly large and coarse, grabbed the back of his shirt collar and dragged him down into the darkness of the basement. Kyle did not resist; his body was on automatic pilot.

The large and powerful thing took him down the steps and around to where it had growled at him. It applied pressure to Kyle's shoulder and the boy knelt in the hard, cold dirt.

Kyle blinked. Almost without realizing he had moved he wiped at the cold sweat on his forehead. As his mind started to focus again he felt himself gulping air. He tried to swallow but his throat was dry. He shivered, felt a cold breeze on his arms and on his face and neck. The thing that had brought him back down to the basement walked in front of him and stood perhaps five feet away. Kyle's eyes must have adjusted to the near-complete darkness because he could see the thing's shape, a shadow among shadows. It was big, *very* big, but it looked to be a man. Except its right hand. It was shaggy and ended in sharp claws.

"Do not be frightened."

It was not the man-thing which spoke. This was a woman's voice. It was sweet, soothing.

Kyle's breathing continued to accelerate. His head swam. He felt as if he might pass out.

Another shadow separated itself from the darkness and stood next to the man-thing. It was clearly a woman but he could see no detail beyond her silhouette.

"Such a scared little boy," she whispered. "But why? We have done nothing to hurt you." She may have placed her hand on the man-thing's arm; it was difficult to tell in the darkness. "We don't want to hurt you. Isn't that right?"

Her companion grunted.

She stepped closer until she stood directly in front of Kyle. Her voice was the delicate purr of a kitten. "In fact, we would like to help you." She knelt in front of Kyle. One of her fingers pressed gently beneath his chin and forced him to look at her.

Kyle recoiled at once. The woman's fingers were cold, so cold his muscles began to shiver. He no longer cared about escaping the basement or finding a way out of the house or even of making it back home to his mother. His list of wishes had dwindled to just one. He never wanted to be touched by this woman again, as long as he lived.

Fearing she might grasp him more forcefully if he did not look at her, he turned his head back in her direction and opened his eyes to just a slit. Kyle still could not make out much in the way of detail but something about the woman made him think of a bird. His eyes focused on hers. They were bright red and devoid of pupils. The woman's lips pulled back from her teeth. It might have been a smile but Kyle was focused on the sharp fangs that revealed themselves.

"We would certainly like to help you, Kyle. Oh, yes, we would. But first, you have to do something for us. What do you say? Do we have a deal?"

Her hands came to rest gently on Kyle's shoulders. They were cold, as if the woman had just come inside after escaping a raging blizzard. Ice crystals formed on his shirt beneath her hands.

Kyle stuttered. From somewhere very far away he heard himself say, "Yes."

"Wonderful," the woman purred. "Let us talk."

Chapter Eight

Three Different Directions, Shawn's Room

As Kyle and Nevaeh were beginning their descent into the basement, Xavier looked through the cracked windows on either side of the front door. The soldiers were still there, standing amid the high grass. He could just make out the top of Andy's head, the boy's hands still clasped behind it. He could not see Mr. Bisaillon, but every few seconds Andy would cast a worried glance beside him. The boy's expression told Xavier their teacher was still there, likely still unconscious. The black birds wheeled through the sky, squawking and cawing. Their pace seemed to have slowed somewhat but their orbit of the property continued uninterrupted.

"What's happening out there?" Maya asked.

"Same thing that was happening before," Xavier replied.

He turned from the windows and regarded the dilapidated staircase. Under any other circumstance Xavier would never trust it. It looked as if it would collapse if someone so much as sneezed near it. But these circumstances were anything but ordinary. Xavier approached it and placed one foot on the bottom step. It creaked but held his weight. He took the second step, ready to spring backward if he felt it giving way. It seemed solid enough. He turned to his classmates.

"We go one at a time. Maya, you follow me, Carlos you go third."

They nodded their agreement. Carlos grumbled at his placement but otherwise there were no objections.

It was slow going up their stairs but after several moments the three students from Mr. Bisaillon's eighth grade class stood on the second floor landing. Two narrow passages led to the right and to the left and a wide hallway lay before them, heading toward the back of the house, if Xavier was any judge of direction.

"Now what?" Maya asked.

"Three different directions, three of us," Xavier replied.

"Okay, I *know* you're not suggesting we should split up. Have you ever even *seen* a scary movie?"

"She has a point," Carlos added.

Xavier frowned. Carlos had tried to sound nonchalant but it was clear he was frightened. Not that Xavier could blame him.

"If you two want to stick together, fine. Pick a direction. Check your cells every minute or so. If you get a signal, shout. I'll do the same."

"Okay," Carlos agreed. "We'll go down there." He indicated the left hallway with a nod of his head.

"Meet back here in ten minutes. Good luck."

Xavier watched them go but only for a moment. He eyed the wide hallway that led toward the back of the house. A large window at the end of the hallway allowed some light through its dust-covered and cracked glass. The hallway on the right sported several doors along the walls but was much darker.

One of those doors might lead to an attic, he thought. *The higher up, the better, if you want to get a signal.* Xavier took the hallway to the right.

The light from that large window all but vanished after he took a few steps. Xavier pulled out his cell and turned it on. His wallpaper image (the Avengers battling Thanos) was bright enough but still managed to provide only limited light. He tried the first door and the knob turned easily in his hand. Xavier pushed the door open.

It looked as if the room might have belonged to a little girl. A small bed, its frame collapsed and its sheets decayed, lay near the far wall. The closet, its doors rotted and hanging by the top hinges, revealed ancient dresses and skirts. Some toys lay scattered about. Xavier checked his cell, tried not to be surprised that he still had no signal.

The door across from the girl's room opened into a bathroom. It was in much the same shape as the rest of the house.

Xavier had to step over a rather large hole in the floor before he made it to the next set of doors. The first was locked. Dust drifted down lazily when he tried the knob. He regarded it and thought he was strong enough to force it open. On the other hand, the door across from it was slightly ajar. He decided on that one, first.

It was once a playroom, that much was obvious. More toys lay scattered about the floor, all covered with dust. Two small bookshelves stood next to each other against the wall to his right. Their shelves had collapsed, dumping their contents onto the floor.

Xavier knelt in the dust and picked up one of the books. The cover was devoid of any picture but the title was *The Pickwick Papers* by Charles Dickens. "The *Christmas Carol* guy?" Xavier turned the book over in his hand and a large chunk of the middle pages full out. Dust plumed up when the pages landed on the floor. Xavier grimaced and waved his hand in front of his face. He had already had enough of this room.

He checked the batter power on his phone once he was again in the hallway. He still had a charge of 82%. "That would be great if I could get a dammed signal," he said to no one.

He reached the next set of doors and paused. Something farther down the hallway caught his eye. He approached another doorway and shined his phone's meager light on it. The door that was once there was gone. At first Xavier thought it must have rotted and fallen inside the room. In fact, pieces of it lay on the floor just across the threshold, but it did not appear as if the door had rotted away. Something about the pattern of the debris suggested something else.

Something smashed this door down. Something big and strong. Xavier gulped. Before he could stop himself he began imagining the strength required to do such a thing. The hairs on his arms stood up straight again, as if mimicking the soldiers standing at attention outside. *Just find a signal and get out of here*, a voice shouted in his head. *That's enough sightseeing.*

"Got that right," Xavier replied to the voice.

For some reason the air smelled better near the doorway. He stepped inside the room.

It was a boy's bedroom. The years since its last occupant had slept in here could not disguise the fact. Despite its ancient appearance Xavier was reminded of his own room at home. Even the layout was similar, although his room was maybe one-quarter the size. One of the windows was open; a light, steady breeze wafted inside and stirred little dust devils to dance on the pitted hardwood. The boy's bed lay on the floor in front of the window. Xavier approached it.

The air was indeed fresher near the window. Xavier stood in front of it and breathed deeply. He had not realized until that moment the smell of decay and age that had overtaken the house since its...what? Change? No, that wasn't the right word. It wasn't big enough to describe what had happened just as the soldiers showed up outside. After a moment, it came to him. It's *transformation*. His English teacher, Mrs. Gauvin, would be proud of him. *Assuming you see her again*, the voice in his head chimed in. "Shut up," Xavier told it. He was starting to dislike that voice.

He peeked outside. The window looked out on the front yard. From this height he could see the assembled soldiers quite clearly. He could also see Andy and Mr. Bisaillon. The teacher had recovered and now knelt in the tall grass with his hands behind his head, the mirror image of Andy.

He cast a nervous eye at the black birds. They seemed much closer than they had from downstairs. He was able to pick out individual birds in the black mass that maintained that tight circle of darkness in the bright blue sky.

Xavier turned his eyes back to Mr. Bisaillon. He wanted to shout something, anything, to get his teacher's attention. He very nearly did.

He stopped himself when it occurred to him he would also draw the attention of the soldiers. The thought of them swinging their rifles toward his window and opening fire killed any thought of trying to shout to Mr. Bisaillon.

Xavier looked at his phone. His lips pursed. He could not do anything to draw the soldiers' attention, but perhaps he was up high enough they would not notice movement in the window. Slowly, expecting the air to erupt in gunfire, Xavier held his phone outside the window. He peeked with one eye at the upper left corner of the screen.

His heart nearly leaped from his chest. The usual message of NO SERVICE was gone, replaced by a single bar. "Oh my God, oh my God," he whispered. Quickly he brought the phone inside and hit the *Recent* icon. The display obediently changed to a list of all the recent numbers he had texted and called. He selected the one labeled MOM and hit it. Nothing happened. No ringing, no elapsed time ticking by. He regarded the phone again. The familiar NO SERVICE message had returned.

Frustrated but not deterred, Xavier again held the phone outside the window.

A high-pitched scream cut through the air. Xavier yelped and jumped back from the window. He felt the phone fly from his fingers and then he was flat on his back. "No!" He scrambled to his feet and all but leaped for the window. He reached it just in time to see his phone disappear into the tall grass below. "No no no *no!*" he shouted.

For an awful moment Xavier pictured himself leaping from the window, following the path of his phone. He could not have lost it, not when he had finally managed to get a signal. He may even have done just that, if not for the soldiers looking up at him and swinging their rifles in his direction.

Xavier cast one long, heartbroken look at the spot where his phone had vanished before he threw himself onto the bed. He curled into a tight ball with his arms covering his head, waiting for the volley of fire to shred the wall next to him.

He did hear several shouts from outside, but the soldiers held their fire. It took several moments for Xavier to realize they were not going to launch a barrage of gunfire in his direction. Slowly, tentatively, he opened up. He dared not look outside again, despite the sudden and continuous clamor that reached his ears. On hands and knees he crawled from the bed. He cast a final look over his shoulder at the window and his lost phone. As he did he bumped into something.

Xavier looked forward. A pair of boots stood directly in front of him. Every muscle in his body froze instantly. *Those boots weren't there a minute ago*, the voice in his head informed him. *No kidding*, Xavier thought back. His eyes moved on their own. They followed the boots up to a pair of blue leggings. Then a black leather belt. On the side of the belt was a long sheath. What could only be a sword handle protruded from that sheath. Xavier's eyes continued their slow climb.

Above the belt was a blue shirt with silver buttons down the center. Two gloved hands hung on either side of the shirt. A single stripe (*a chevron*, the voice informed him, *remember? From Miss DiBella's second marking period history class?*) adorned each sleeve near the shoulder. Atop it all was the face of the man inside the uniform.

Man? A kid, maybe only a year or two older than Xavier. The kid-soldier looked down upon him, his face expressionless.

The world suddenly swam out of focus. Xavier felt his arms buckle and then his cheek rested upon the cold hardwood of a little boy's bedroom. He remembered nothing after that.

Chapter Nine

Andy Seizes An Opportunity

Nevaeh made it through the cellar door and back into the kitchen. She paused only a moment to see if Kyle was coming but she could hear nothing from the absolute darkness that was the old house's basement. She turned in the direction of the foyer but she stopped when her eyes fixed upon the fallen refrigerator. Some of the letter magnets were back on the refrigerator door. At first her mind refused to comprehend the message before she came to the conclusion one of the others had decided to have a bit of fun at her expense. NO S RVIC , the letter magnets informed her. Her eyes lingered only a moment on the message before she bolted for the foyer.

When she reached it she looked at the top of the twin staircases and shouted, "Xavier! Carlos! Maya! Hey, you guys, something's in the basement! I think it got Kyle!" Her voice echoed off the walls. It sounded shrill and nearly incomprehensible to her ears.

"Guys!" She waited. None of her friends appeared at the top of the stairs. No one came running to see what she was screaming about. Nevaeh ran for the stairs but stopped short. They looked as if they might come crashing down if she took them at full speed. Something from Mrs. Rizzo's science class about the weight of an object increasing the faster it moved. Nevaeh wished she had paid closer attention to the lesson.

And yet…If whatever was in the basement came up after her, she would be better off with the others. She placed one foot on the bottom step. It creaked but held. Slowly, her arms stretched out to either side like a high wire artist, Nevaeh began to ascend the stairs.

Rough, strong hands clamped down upon her shoulders and yanked her back. Nevaeh screamed.

****

Carlos was getting tired of dead-ends. He was also getting tired of the same message on his cell. "I give up," he announced to Maya as they exited the fourth room. "We're never gonna get a signal up here. Maybe if we find the attic we'll have more luck."

Maya shrugged. "Maybe Xavier already did," she offered. "Maybe help is already on the way."

"Maybe," Carlos agreed, but he did not think so. Even if Xavier had managed to get a signal and make a call, they were in the middle of nowhere. Unless the cops were coming in a jet plane the students of Mr. Bisaillon's eighth grade class likely were on their own for the night. He said none of this to Maya, of course. No reason to make her any more scared than she was already. Not that he was feeling particularly brave, either. He pointed to the next door in line. "Let's try another one."

The door fell into the room as soon as Carlos touched the knob. Maya yelped and jumped back. Dust billowed into the hallway and around their feet. The sound echoed off the walls, sounding like the fading heartbeat of a dying giant.

"Sorry," Maya said sheepishly.

"It's cool," Carlos replied. He waved away the dust and peered inside the room.

It was large, with multiple windows overlooking the front of the house. Several pieces of furniture stood beneath white sheets, deformed ghosts standing guard over dust and cobwebs.

Carlos strode carefully but quickly toward the closest window, his phone held in front of him. Still no signal. It occurred to him he might have better luck if he opened the window and held the phone outside. It was unlikely to produce the desired result but their luck had to change sooner or later. He looked through the dusty glass.

He got a bird's-eye view of the front yard. The soldiers stood in formation, standing guard over Andy and Mr. Bisaillon. They knelt in the high grass next to each other, hands folded behind their head. "I can see Andy and Mr. Bisaillon."

"Are they okay?" Maya asked from the doorway.

"I think so. Hard to tell from here. They're alive, anyway."

He stopped short when he saw the birds. "Oh, wow. Oh, jeez!" He regretted saying anything.

Maya stepped next to him and looked outside. Her hands went to her mouth. They undoubtedly helped the girl stifle a scream but her sharp intake of breath was enough for Carlos.

He placed his hands gently onto the girl's shoulders and moved her away from the window. Her feet shuffled slowly on the rotted floor; her hands remained clamped over her mouth. "It's cool, Maya, it's cool. Just stand back a bit. I have an idea." Carlos tried the window. It may as well have been welded shut. "Here, take this." He held his phone out to Maya.

The girl seemed reluctant to remove her hands from her mouth, as if doing so would unleash the scream she was trying so hard to suppress. In the end she steadied herself. She took the phone and put it into her jacket pocket.

Carlos gripped the bottom of the window with both hands and lifted with everything he had. It refused to budge. He lost his grip and his fingernails raked up the bottom of the frame and across the glass. Carlos shook his hands. "Dammit! That hurt!" He looked about the room. "Screw this."

He strode to one of the white sheets and pulled it away. A tall floor lamp stood revealed. "Perfect." He picked it up and approached the window.

"Wait, they'll see!" Maya shouted.

"Like they don't know we're in here already." He swung the lamp with everything he had.

The window glass shattered. So did the lamp post. Half of it dangled outside the window, held together by the thin, ancient wires within. Carlos started to haul it back inside.

The scream was distant but loud. Carlos, startled, dropped the floor lamp; it disappeared outside the window.

"That was Nevaeh!" Maya shouted. She started for the door, stopped, looked at Carlos.

Carlos took a step toward the door but stopped when he saw what was happening outside.

The soldiers, their eyes drawn to the house either by the smashed window or the scream, took their attention from their captives. Mr. Bisaillon sprang to his feet and grabbed the soldier nearest him. He managed to wrest the rifle away from the man and he swung it like Aaron Judge with the bases loaded. The butt of the rifle connected solidly with the soldier's head and the man stumbled back and disappeared into the tall grass. At the same time Mr. Bisaillon shouted something to Andy. The blonde kid jumped to his feet and bolted for the front doors.

"We have to get down there, now!" Carlos exclaimed.

He ran from the room, not looking but assuming Maya was on his heels. "Xavier!" Carlos shouted as they reached the wide area at the top of the twin staircases. He could see nothing down the right hallway, no sign his friend was coming or had even heard him.

There was a commotion in the foyer. Nevaeh was slapping at Kyle. James Buchannan Middle School's resident bad boy grabbed at Nevaeh's arms in a move to protect himself but he had as yet not struck back at the girl.

Carlos flew down the steps. He made it about two-thirds of the way before the sharp crack of splintering wood filled the foyer. One of the steps disintegrated beneath his feet. For a brief moment he was weightless, suspended in the air, before gravity returned and plunged him into the hole vacated by the old wood. His arms shot out and he caught himself on the steps above and below him before his entire body disappeared into the darkness.

Maya shouted something and ran for him. Try as he might Carlos could not free himself from the hole. The jagged edges of splintered wood cut his skin and tore at his shirt. Maya reached him and grabbed one of his arms and pulled for all she was worth.

Above the sound of Maya's struggles and the battle between Nevaeh and Kyle, Carlos heard something else. Pounding, frantic pounding, coming from the front door. "Someone get the dammed door!" he shouted. "Andy and Mr. B are trying to come in!"

Maya ceased her rescue attempt. Nevaeh and even Kyle stopped their struggle. All three looked at him, clearly surprised.

"Open the door *now*!" Carlos shouted.

The pounding on the door was accompanied by shouting, but Carlos could not make out any specific words. The voice on the other side of the door was frantic, even panicked, too scared to form coherent words, let alone sentences.

Kyle started for the door.

Nevaeh grabbed his arm. "Wait! What if it's a trick?"

He pulled his arm from her and grasped both door handles.

"Let them in!" Carlos pleaded.

Kyle pulled both handles, grunting with the effort and straining his muscles. To everyone's surprise the doors flew open.

Andy rocketed inside so quickly he crossed the foyer and crashed into one of the old writing tables. Kyle lost all semblance of balance and tumbled backward. He crashed into Nevaeh and sent the girl sprawling. Kyle kept his feet under him somehow and raced back to the doors. Whatever he saw caused him to slam both doors closed with as much force as he could muster.

"Mr. Bisaillon!" Carlos shouted. "What about Mr. Bisaillon?"

Kyle put his back to the doors and planted himself there. The doors jumped in their frame as something on the other side tried to get in.

Kyle held his ground, gritting his teeth with each new impact. After a moment whatever was out there gave up. The pounding stopped.

Carlos, with Maya's help, finally managed to extricate himself from the hole in the stairs. His shirt was torn and he had deep scratches on his arms and abdomen. There was blood but not much. He decided the wounds weren't likely to be fatal. He made his way carefully down to the foyer, Maya in tow.

Nevaeh was helping Andy to his feet. The blonde boy looked dazed but otherwise unhurt. Kyle remained with his back to the door, breathing heavy. Carlos looked at him, into his eyes.

Kyle returned the stare but only for a moment. Then he looked away.

Chapter Ten

A New Message, A Betrayal

Carlos ran for the front doors and looked out the windows. There were a lot of gray- and blue-shirted soldiers on the front deck. They were moving off, now, some of the officers shouting orders to them. He could see no sign of Mr. Bisaillon.

"Andy, what happened to Mr. B?" Carlos asked, turning away from the window.

The new arrival was unsteady on his feet, alternately leaning against the wall and Nevaeh. He shook his head every few moments like a cartoon character who had just taken a pounding in the boxing ring. Finally he looked at Carlos, his expression entirely uncomprehending.

"Huh?"

"Mr. Bisaillon! Where is he? What happened out there?"

"He was right behind me."

"Well, he ain't there now," Kyle said, his back still against the door.

Carlos looked at the bigger boy. "You didn't..." His voice trailed off. No, no way. Kyle Reed was a jerk, the biggest jerk in the school and destined for low-paying menial jobs for the rest of his life, yes. But even *he* wasn't capable of that.

"Didn't *what*?" Kyle was back to his usual angry self in an instant.

"Forget it," Carlos told him.

"Damn right, forget it." Kyle stepped away from the door, peeked through the window.

"You okay?" Carlos asked, turning his attention to Andy.

Andy nodded and immediately grimaced. "Head hurts, but yeah, I guess so. Wait a minute. Something happened. Those guys in the Civil War getup looked like they were about to shoot at the house.

Then there was a scream. They got distracted and that's when Mr. Bisaillon grabbed one of them. Then we ran for it."

"They must have caught Mr. B," Nevaeh stated matter-of-factly.

"Thanks, Captain Obvious," Kyle remarked.

Nevaeh took an angry step in Kyle's direction. Carlos got between them and stopped her. "We can't fight with each other, not now, anyway. Save it for when we get outta here."

Nevaeh glared at Kyle but the fight seemed to have left her. She turned and walked to Maya. Both girls kept their silence.

"What did you find in the basement?" Carlos asked Kyle. "Anything?"

"Not much, just a lot of old junk," Kyle replied.

"And a big dog," Nevaeh added. When Carlos looked at her questioningly, she continued, "Or something. I don't know what it was. Some kind of animal. I heard it growl."

Carlos glanced at Kyle.

The bigger boy shrugged. "I didn't hear nothin'. We were checking the place out and then she freaked and ran. Left me all alone down there. *Alone* being the important word in that sentence. No wild animals, no nothin'."

"You liar!" Nevaeh shouted. "There *was* an animal or something down there! I heard it!"

"Whatever," Kyle remarked. He kicked at a stray piece of rotted wood on the floor.

"And where's my phone? You had it."

"I dropped it. Maybe that wild animal of yours ate it."

Nevaeh glowered at him. Her mouth worked but she seemed too angry to speak at that moment. Maya placed a comforting hand on her arm.

"We'll get the phone later," Carlos assured the angry girl. "For now I still have mine. And Xavier—" Carlos's eyes widened. "Oh, man, where's Xavier?"

"Probably hiding under a bed somewhere," Kyle sneered.

Carlos craned his neck toward the second floor. "Xavier!" The walls threw echoes of his voice in every direction. Carlos tried again. He could hear nothing from the second floor. "We have to go find him."

"Uh-uh, no way," Nevaeh told him. "I ain't going nowhere. We're waiting right here for someone to come get us." She checked with Maya. The other girl nodded silently.

Carlos's lips pressed into a thin line. "Fine, stay here. Keep a close watch on those guys outside. See if you can spot Mr. Bisaillon. Kyle and I will look for—"

"Whoa, whoa, whoa." Kyle held up both hands. "I don't even like the little jerk. And since when do I take orders from you, Medina? Suddenly you're the teacher now?"

Carlos nearly began another argument but he stopped himself. What was the point? "Okay, you can stay here. With the *girls*. Me and Andy will go upstairs. You game?"

Andy stopped rubbing the back of his head long enough to give Carlos a thumbs-up.

"We'll find Xavier and come right back down," Carlos told Nevaeh and Maya. "Hang tight."

****

Nevaeh watched the two boys ascend the right staircase to the second floor. One of the steps creaked loudly and she was certain it would give way, plunging both boys to who-knew-where. Carlos and Andy sprinted up the last few steps and made it to the second floor landing. Carlos waved. Nevaeh waved back. Then he and Andy were gone from her sight.

Kyle turned to them. "Sorry I dropped your phone. Wanna go find it?" His voice was calm, even soothing, very unKyle-like. Even his expression was soft.

"Are you serious?"

Kyle shrugged. "The only two phones are upstairs now. Wouldn't you feel better if you had yours back?"

She would. Nevaeh glanced at Maya. Her friend looked reluctant, to say the least. "He has a point," Neveah told her. "What if…" She was about to say, *What if they don't come back?* but she stopped herself. "What if I get home and my mom's really mad at me for losing it? She'll ground me for a month."

"Neveah, I don't know…"

"Please!" Nevaeh was surprised at how much she wanted to get her phone back. It had nothing to do with the possibility of being grounded for losing it; she was suddenly convinced she would never see Xavier and the other boys again. This house was going to swallow them up and never spit them out. That meant her phone was the only chance they had left of calling for help. It really was that simple. "Please," she repeated, her tone soft.

Maya looked down the hallway leading to the kitchen. Then at Kyle. Then back to Nevaeh. "Okay, fine. We'll get your phone."

Nevaeh smiled. "Thank you."

Kyle led the way back to the kitchen. There was still plenty of daylight left, judging by the meager light that managed to get through the grime and dust on the windows. Kyle strode to the nearest window and peeked outside. His body language told Nevaeh all she needed to know about what he saw in the back yard.

She took a single step in the direction of the door which led to the basement. She froze when her eyes fell upon the refrigerator. The letter magnets spelled out a different message than before. It read: TH IDOL IS TH K Y.

"What's that mean?" Maya asked when she followed her friend's gaze.

Nevaeh turned to Kyle. "You need to knock that off," she hissed. "Stop trying to scare me!"

Kyle turned away from the window. "What are you talking about?" Some of his usual belligerence had returned to his voice since the foyer.

Nevaeh pointed to the fridge. "That. Stop leaving me your little love notes on the fridge. It ain't funny."

Kyle looked at the refrigerator door and his brow furrowed. He appeared confused but only for a moment. Then he shrugged. "Sorry. Thought I'd play around with ya a little. My bad."

"Just don't do it anymore," Nevaeh told him. She pointed to the basement door. "You gonna go get it or what?"

"*We* are gonna go get it," Kyle replied.

Nevaeh expected as much. "Okay. But you dropped it so you go first. We'll follow you."

"Bunch of wussies around here," Kyle mumbled. He strode to the door purposefully and grasped the handle. He yanked it open quite suddenly and with far more force than was necessary. He peered inside. "See? No wild animals, no monsters, no nothing." He took a step toward the threshold.

He spun so quickly Nevaeh never saw it coming. The large boy grabbed Maya's arm and threw her toward the open door. The girl screamed and disappeared into the darkness. Nevaeh heard the unmistakable sound of her friend tumbling down the steps. "*Maya!*" Nevaeh ran to the open door.

Rough hands planted themselves on her back and shoved. Nevaeh lost all semblance of balance. Her hand brushed against the rail but only for a split-second, not long enough for her to grab it. She hit the first step, then the second, each impact sending lightning bolts throughout her body. She fell for what seemed like hours until she finally came to a stop at the bottom of the stairs. She had landed on something soft; it took her only a moment to realize it was her friend.

"Maya? You okay?"

A weak whimper, barely audible, was the only reply she received.

"Someone wants to meet you," she heard Kyle say from somewhere far away.

Nevaeh looked up the stairs. Kyle stood silhouetted in the doorway. She could not see his face but she knew he was smiling.

"Have fun!" He slammed the door closed.

The darkness of the basement became absolute. Nevaeh felt about until she found the first step. Before she could even attempt the stairs she had to extricate herself from Maya. Her friend had yet to say anything. Nevaeh did not know if the girl was even conscious.

"Such sweet, pretty little girls," a woman's voice purred from the darkness.

Every muscle in Nevaeh's body locked up. Unable to move, unable to speak, her eyes turned in the direction of the voice. She could see nothing, of course, but she knew whomever was down here with them was coming closer. She thought she could hear footsteps drawing closer to her, but it might have been her own heartbeat. It thundered in her ears and threatened to drown out all other sound in the world.

The basement had gotten colder since she had ventured down here with Kyle. It seemed to radiate from the floor, the walls, everything. She told herself it was for this reason alone her muscles began to quiver.

Then, quite suddenly, she could see something. *Two* somethings, it turned out. They were small and red and they were definitely approaching her. And still she could not move a muscle.

The two red somethings became a pair of eyes. They emerged from the darkness of the basement, becoming brighter as their owner drew closer. The woman knelt in the dirt next to the two girls. Nevaeh felt the woman's hand beneath her chin, lifting up her head as if to get a better look at her. Nevaeh recoiled and gasped at the woman's frigid touch. The hand may as well have been sculpted from ice. Her chin went numb immediately.

"Very pretty indeed." Her voice was soft velvet, like a movie star's from the 1940s. "And I have so many things to show you."

The woman stood. Somehow, despite the complete darkness, Nevaeh knew the woman had spread her arms wide. She also became aware that the woman was not alone. There was someone else down here. Or some*thing*. And it was big.

"Help them to their feet," the woman ordered.

Something that felt very much like the paw of a giant animal settled under Nevaeh's arm. She felt herself being lifted into the air.

Nevaeh found her voice at last. She screamed.

Chapter Eleven

The Messengers, Andy Takes A Spill

"Did you hear that?"

Carlos paused in the hallway. He and Andy had just exited the third room in their so-far-fruitless search for Xavier.

"Hear what?"

"Shh!" Carlos held up his hand and listened intently. Aside from his own breathing he could hear nothing. He shook his head. "I don't know. I thought I heard something from downstairs. Then again, it might have been from outside, too. This house does something weird to sounds."

"I didn't hear anything," Andy told him.

Carlos shook his head again. "It was probably nothing. Let's keep going."

The next door was locked. Carlos was about to knock, stopped himself. *That would be ridiculous*, he thought. Instead, he shouted, "Xavier? You in there?" He put his ear to the door but no sound came from the other side. He looked at Andy. "You're bigger. See if you can get it open."

Andy appeared reluctant. "You sure about that?"

"Yes," Carlos lied. In point of fact he was not sure he wanted to see the room on the other side of the door. But it was possible Xavier ran inside and locked it behind him. *Especially if something was chasing him.* "Give it a try."

Andy turned the doorknob. When that didn't produce any results he threw his shoulder into the door. Dust drifted down from the top of the doorframe. The bigger boy coughed and waved it away. He stepped back, then charged at the obstinate door. The wood cracked but the door held. Andy bounced a few feet back. He rubbed his shoulder, looked at Carlos. "Well, that's not opening."

Carlos frowned. "Let's try it together."

The two boys walked back to the opposite wall. They each cast a sideways glance at the other. Then they surged forward.

This time the door shattered under their combined assault. The boys' momentum carried them into the room. Their legs became entangled with one another's and they sprawled onto the floor. The breath exploded from Carlos's lungs. He gasped air, tried to separate himself from his classmate. It took him only a moment and he rolled clear of Andy. He came up sputtering for breath.

His hands and arms were scraped. Pinpricks of blood blossomed on his palms. He rubbed them absently on his pants. When he saw what was in front of him, his breath hitched in his throat and his muscles froze.

Two children stood in front of him and Andy. They were clearly brother and sister. The boy looked to be no more than a year or two younger than Carlos, while the girl was a few years younger than her brother. They did not move, did not speak. They simply looked at the two new arrivals, their expressions blank.

"Who...Who..." Carlos found he could not speak.

"Whoa!" Andy had finally noticed the two kids. He scrambled backwards on his hands and knees toward the now-open doorway. "Carlos! Let's go!"

Carlos found he still could not move. He looked at the kids and they looked at him.

The idol, the boy said without moving his lips. *The idol is the key*.

The little girl appeared to stiffen when her brother spoke. She looked about nervously and tugged on his arm.

Find the idol, the boy continued.

The girl became more frantic. Her eyes flitted about every corner of the room as if she was expecting something bad to happen. *Shawn,* she pleaded. Like her brother she spoke without moving her lips.

"Come on, man, let's go!" Andy shouted from just outside the room.

Carlos realized he had regained some of his ability to move. He glanced over his shoulder at Andy. Just as quickly he whipped his head back to the two children.

They were gone. Carlos was alone inside the room. He looked about but there was nothing within the room that was large enough for two children to hide behind. Not that they could have moved more than a foot or two in the time his head was turned.

Where are their footprints? Carlos gasped. The dust on the floor where the children stood was undisturbed. He looked at the floor around him for confirmation. He had left easily visible footprints in the dust. The two younger kids had not.

"What just happened?" he asked when his voice returned from its brief vacation. "You did see them, right?"

"Oh, I saw them," Andy replied from the hallway. "Can we go now?"

Carlos got to his feet and looked about the room again, as if his eyes deceived him and the two kids were still there. But they were not. He swallowed hard and joined Andy in the hallway. "Let's find Xavier and get back to the others."

Carlos glanced down the hallway and counted doors. "Three more...No, wait. That one at the end, it doesn't have a door. Let's try that one."

Before the two boys could take a step they heard Kyle from downstairs shout, "Hey, morons! Get down here. Nevaeh got hurt. She needs your help!"

Carlos and Andy exchanged glances. As much as Carlos needed to find Xavier he could not ignore Nevaeh if she was hurt. Carlos read

Andy's eyes and knew his friend had reached the same conclusion. The two kids who disappeared in front of him temporarily forgotten, Carlos said, "Come on!" They took off back the way they had come.

They took the stairs two at a time despite the groans they received from the decayed wood. Kyle stood in the foyer watching their progress.

"What happened?" Andy asked when they reached the bottom.

"How do I Know?" Kyle replied. "The idiot probably tripped over something in the basement when we were looking for her phone. Can't see much of anything down there. But she's hurt pretty bad."

Andy set off down the hallway which led to the kitchen. Kyle followed him. Carlos remained in the foyer a moment, watching them. Something wasn't right, he didn't know what. It was about Nevaeh and Kyle, that much he knew, but he couldn't figure it out. Whatever it was it remained annoyingly out of his reach, like an itch he simply couldn't scratch. With a frown he followed the other two boys into the kitchen.

When he arrived Kyle had taken position to the side of the basement door, pointing. Andy stood at the threshold, looking down into darkness.

"Nevaeh? Maya? Where are you?"

"I already told you, dummy. They're down there."

Andy frowned at Kyle. He returned his attention to the basement. "Nevaeh? Can you hear me? You okay?"

"They're as okay as they're gonna be," Kyle told him. Then he shoved Andy through the opening.

Carlos rushed forward. He could hear Andy tumbling down the stairs, hear the boy's grunts of pain, and then a crash as he must have hit the bottom.

"Andy!" Carlos had every intention of going after him. In his haste he forgot about Kyle.

The larger boy slammed his elbow into Carlos's stomach. Carlos gulped and doubled over. Kyle threw the basement door shut and turned in his direction. Carlos dropped to one knee. He pushed himself back as the other boy advanced on him. He gulped air, blinked the tears from his eyes.

"Where's…" He found it difficult to speak.

"Nevaeh?" Kyle replied. "Who cares? She's down there somewhere. So is Maya. I suspect Andy will be seeing them real soon. You will, too. And then Valsaint. I can't wait to get my hands on him."

Carlos continued to push himself backward. He felt something behind him. It was the fallen refrigerator. He froze when he saw the letter magnets arranged into a sentence: FIND TH IDOL.

Kyle loomed over him. Both hands were curled into fists. "She said she wants all of you. If I help her she'll let me go." He knelt down until he was eye-level with Carlos. "That's a hell of a deal if you ask me."

Carlos's hand found the refrigerator door handle. It was an inch or two above the floor and hanging from the door by a single screw. He grasped it and hoped it would hold.

"Oh, and you were right, before. Bisaillon almost made it inside. I slammed the door in his face and it felt *awesome*! I wanted to do something like that all year!" Kyle threw his head back and laughed. "Let those Civil War actors outside have him. I think *she* prefers kids, anyway." He ruffled Carlos's hair. "Time to say good night, Medina."

"Good night." Carlos lifted the refrigerator door with everything he had, gasping at the pain it produced in his abdomen. The thing flew open and up. It caught Kyle squarely in the jaw and sent the larger boy stumbling backward. The letter magnets sailed through the air in all directions. Kyle crashed into the counter and bounced off. He landed hard on the floor and rolled.

Carlos pushed himself to his feet. Still holding a hand over his bruised abdomen he staggered from the kitchen. He dropped to one knee a few feet from the foyer, gasping. He could hear Kyle moaning and swearing in the kitchen and knew it would be only a few moments before James Buchannan Middle School's Bully Number One would be on him again. That thought alone was enough to get Carlos back on his feet. There were certain things all kids knew not to do to live a long, healthy life. Hitting Kyle Reed in the face with a refrigerator door was pretty high on that list. In fact, right now, it was at the top.

Carlos emerged into the foyer, intending to get back up to the second floor. If he could find Xavier before Kyle found him, the two of them together might be enough to handle the bigger boy.

He cast a glance over his shoulder, expecting to see Kyle rocketing up the hallway. As yet there was no sign of him. That was good. Carlos needed as much of a head start as possible. He turned back toward the twin staircases...

And ran directly into Xavier.

Chapter Twelve

Xavier Learns A Few Things

The kid in the blue military uniform extended his hand. Xavier swallowed. The last thing in the world he wanted to do was accept that hand. It would mean touching the kid, and Xavier doubted he would find that a pleasant experience. He eyed the rifle slung over the kid's shoulder. *Well, that pretty much eliminates the possibility of running away*, he thought. Seeing no other option, Xavier accepted the offered hand. It was cold but not as cold as Xavier expected. The kid soldier pulled him to his feet and then stood back.

"You're a ghost, right?" Xavier asked the boy.

A spirit, yes, the kid said without moving his lips. He snapped off a salute. *Private Caleb Mason, at your service, sir.*

"Nice to meet you." It was all Xavier could think to say.

You and your friends are in very serious trouble, I'm afraid, Caleb continued, still without moving his lips. *In fact, I'd say you've never been in this much trouble in your whole life.*

Xavier rubbed the back of his neck. "We're trapped in a house that's surrounded by some weird army guys and we can't call for help. So, yeah, we're in trouble."

Caleb smirked and nodded. *But that's not the worst of it. If you ever want to see your family again you have to know what's happening, and what came before. I can show you, if you'll let me.*

Xavier took an involuntary step back. Although this kid had done him no harm, and seemed decidedly non-hostile, by his own admission he was a ghost. That meant he was dead. *Then again, with everything that's happened today, is* this *where you draw the line?* Xavier willed the voice in his head to shut up. He was not comforted by the idea that the voice was right.

"I guess," he said at last.

Caleb extended his hand again. Xavier looked at it again, quite skeptically, then slowly placed his hand in the dead boy's.

There was a *whoosh* and Xavier felt the bile rising up in his throat. It was similar to the sensation he received when the house transformed around them. The world whipped past him far too quickly for him to see anything other than a blur. There was sound, as well, a cacophony that assaulted his ears even after he covered them with his hands. The rollercoaster feeling returned, much more powerful than it had been earlier. This time Xavier felt he was close to losing consciousness. He wanted to tell Caleb to stop but his voice died in his throat. Or perhaps he was screaming at the top of his lungs. There was no way to know.

And then the world slammed back into focus. Xavier gasped for breath, afraid to lift his head or even open his eyes. He was outside someplace; the dirt and grass beneath him told him that much. The sound that had filled his world only a moment before was gone, replaced with shouts and cries and the unmistakable crack of gunshots. Xavier shook his head to clear it. Slowly, with the utmost reluctance, he opened his eyes.

He found himself in the middle of a battle. Soldiers in blue uniforms fought others wearing gray. Some fought hand-to-hand, some swung their rifles at each other, but most were firing their weapons at the enemy. Men and boys fell all around him. No, not him, *them*. Caleb surveyed the battle, a curiously detached expression etched into his features. After a few moments he seemed to remember Xavier was next to him. Again, he offered his hand. This time Xavier waved him off and stood on his own. Touching the boy soldier twice was more than enough for Xavier. He looked about.

The battle was not going well for the blue coats. Xavier saw many of them, most of them, lying about the ground. A few struggled weakly to crawl away but most were still as statues. The gray coats were firing their rifles and surging forward. Although he could hear their rifle shots as well as the screams of the dying, he could smell nothing. He felt he should be grateful for that.

That these men and boys were dressed identically to the soldiers presently holding Mr. Bisaillon and Andy at the business end of their rifles was not lost on Xavier.

Here we come, Caleb informed him. When Xavier gave him a confused look, Caleb pointed down the hill.

One of the blue coats was running in their direction, being pulled by his arm by a very large Indian man with a bear claw instead of a right hand. As they drew nearer, Xavier gasped in surprise. The blue coat was Caleb. He did not know the boy's companion but his mind suddenly flashed back to the thing he had glimpsed in the woods as they walked along the driveway. Although he did not know how, Xavier knew this was what he had seen in the shadows, stalking them.

I never knew his real name. Or maybe it really was Black Bear. Let's follow them, Caleb suggested.

Not seeing as he had a choice, Xavier followed the ghost.

Caleb—the *live* Caleb—and his very large companion stopped running when they crested the hill. The Indian knelt and rummaged through his satchel. Caleb swung his rifle up and aimed it back the way they had come. As yet the gray coats were busying themselves with whoever remained of their enemy but the boy's expression told Xavier he knew what was coming.

Xavier's eyes were drawn to the Indian. His hand emerged from his satchel with something roughly the size of a bowling ball, although it was not round. It was black, the darkest shade of black Xavier had ever seen. He could not make out what it was, although something about it suggested the form of a bird.

The Indian used his bear claw to tear up the ground. Dirt flew in all directions. Some of it passed through Xavier's body as if he himself were a ghost. When Black Bear was satisfied with the size and depth of the hole he placed the black thing inside it and mumbled something Xavier could not hear.

The gray coats were charging up the hill toward them. Black Bear stood and hurled himself at them. Live-Caleb stood, apparently as stunned as was Xavier, at the Indian's savage attack. The gray coats seemed unable to aim their weapons at him, so swiftly did he move. Eventually, however, their numbers won out and Black Bear disappeared beneath a crushing wave of gray uniforms.

Look, ghost-Caleb told him, and pointed.

Xavier looked.

At first he thought it was smoke. Something poured from the hole Black Bear had dug into the earth. The smoke expanded and thickened until Xavier could not see through it. Something moved within the smoke, within the *darkness*. Xavier thought it was a woman, although something about her also reminded him of a bird. What could only have been her eyes snapped open. They were bright red and focused on the men still struggling with Black Bear. The woman and her accompanying zone of darkness surged past Xavier and ghost-Caleb, directly into the mass of soldiers.

At the same time the sky suddenly darkened. Xavier's eyes were drawn upward. Black birds, thousands of them, surged through the air as if they were a single animal. They moved so quickly toward the gray coats Xavier imagined he could feel the wind generated by their flight.

She is Tah-tah-Kro'-ah, *the raven queen, although I did not know it at the time,* ghost-Caleb told him. *She is the last of five sisters who once roamed this world. The natives both worshipped and feared them.* He indicated the soldiers with a nod of his head. *She did what she and her sisters have done since the world was new. She took them all, those who were still living, anyway. This part you probably don't need to see.* He placed his hand over Xavier's eyes.

At first Xavier struggled to get rid of the dead boy's hand, but after a moment of listening to the screams of the surprised soldiers, he decided Caleb was right. He most definitely did not need to see this.

When Caleb lowered his hand Xavier saw all of the gray coats were down. The woman knelt in the dirt beside Black Bear. She seemed to be speaking to him. After a moment the big Indian rose to his feet. He bled from a number of wounds but he seemed unbothered by them. His eyes, too, were red, although they lacked the intensity of the woman's. He began to stride back up the hill, toward live-Caleb.

Xavier turned quickly to his companion. "What is he doing?"

You don't need to see this, either, ghost-Caleb told him.

And then the world spun out of focus and Xavier was back aboard the rollercoaster again.

This time the sensation of being weightless and whipping through space was shorter, although just as violent and unsettling. The sudden stop sent Xavier sprawling onto a hard surface.

"There has to be a better way of doing this," he mumbled. He pushed himself to his knees, willing his stomach to settle down, and looked about.

He was back inside the house, in the living room. The room itself had changed since he last saw it. The furniture was new and clean, the walls adorned with some family photos and paintings. Xavier could hear crickets chirping in the darkness outside.

A woman sat in one of the chairs. A single candle next to her provided the only light within the room but somehow Xavier could see everything quite clearly. She sat and knitted but something about her movements made him uneasy. They were precise, robotic, as if her mind were a million miles away.

Her name was Mrs. Meijer, Caleb informed him. *Her husband built the house in 1881. He passed away a few years later, leaving her to raise their three boys alone.*

At the mention of children Xavier realized he could hear them playing upstairs. Or perhaps not playing. What he took at first to be playful shouting now sounded more like panic. He looked again at Mrs. Meijer. "Something's wrong. Doesn't she hear them?"

Caleb shrugged. *I suppose, on some level. But the raven queen has a way of clouding the senses of adults. They hear, but they don't hear. See, but not see.*

"They're in trouble!" Xavier exclaimed. He made for the staircase, but stopped short when Caleb appeared suddenly in front of him.

I would spare you what lies upstairs.

More sounds from the three Meijer children. Xavier was close enough now that he knew those were not the sounds of play. Something very bad was happening on the second floor. He tried to run through the ghost-boy but Caleb was solid enough that Xavier could not get past him.

"We have to help them!"

We cannot. What you're hearing happened before your great-grandfather was born. It cannot be altered by any means we possess.

Xavier tried again to shoulder his way past Caleb, and again he was unsuccessful. In frustration he turned back toward the living room. "Why isn't she doing something? Is she deaf?"

I told you, she is aware of what's happening, but that realization is buried deep down inside of her. She cannot help her sons. He sounded both sad and resigned.

From upstairs Xavier could hear a woman's voice. It was soft and thick, like poisoned honey. "I have such things to show you," the voice said.

Xavier swallowed hard. "You were right. I don't want to see this."

Caleb placed his hand on Xavier's arm. The room blurred and they were flying again.

When he landed this time he found himself in the room where his journey with Caleb began. They were still in the past, judging by the near-pristine condition of the room.

Two children stood by the window. The older of the two, a boy, looked down, as if judging the distance to the ground below. His younger sister sat on the bed and cried. Something pounded on the door, something *big* from the sound of it. Xavier could guess what it was.

This is Shawn and Maureen Sullivan, Caleb told him.

"And we can't help them, either." It was not a question. He turned quickly on Caleb. "Why are you showing me all this if we can't do anything to help them?"

Because it can help you and your friends, the ghost replied.

The door exploded and sent splinters flying throughout the room. Instinctively Xavier shielded himself before he remembered the splinters could not harm him. The shadowy bulk of Black Bear stood silhouetted within the doorframe. The Sullivan children screamed.

"Get me out of here," Xavier stated flatly. "I don't want to see any more."

Caleb looked at him, nodded once.

The bedroom and the Sullivan children vanished. When Xavier next opened his eyes he was back inside the room. He was no longer in the past; a single look about what was once Shawn Sullivan's bedroom told him they were back in the present. Caleb stood silently next to him.

"So now what?" Xavier asked.

The idol that summoned the raven queen still lies where Black Bear buried it, Caleb replied. *If you ever wish to see your family again you must destroy it.*

"Oh, is that all?" Xavier was too tired to keep the desperation out of his tone. "And how do I do that, exactly?"

To destroy a spectral object you need a spectral weapon.

"Okay, I'll just run down to Target. Be right back."

I fear I do not know what that means, Caleb replied. *But there is something within this house you can use.*

Xavier snapped his fingers. "Your rifle!"

Caleb shook his head. *It is as non-corporeal as am I. You need something that exists in this world, not the spirit world.*

Now it was Xavier's turn to shake his head. "I don't know. I just don't know."

Caleb said, *I can tell you but you will not like it.*

Xavier threw his hands in the air. "Go ahead, tell me."

Caleb told him.

Xavier did not like it.

Chapter Thirteen

Xavier Meets the Raven Queen

"Xavier! Where the heck have you been? We looked all over for you!"

Carlos nearly hugged him. He restrained himself when he remembered who was likely to join them in the foyer at any moment. He cast a quick glance over his shoulder toward the kitchen but Kyle had yet to show himself.

"We have to hide! Reed threw Andy into the cellar. I think he did the same thing to the girls, too. He's working with whatever is creeping around down there. And he'll be here any second."

Xavier waved him off. "Listen, I have a plan to get us out of this, but you have to do what I say."

Hope, the first real hope Carlos felt since the house changed around them, flashed across his eyes. "Okay, what is it?"

Xavier told him as much of what he learned as he felt Carlos would believe. He made no mention of Caleb and shied away from questions about the Sullivan kids. He ended with, "Keep Reed busy. Get him as far from the basement as you can."

Carlos' face fell. "You're kidding."

"No time to argue. Do it!"

Carlos thought this was the perfect time to argue. He opened his mouth to do just that when he heard Kyle Reed curse loudly from down the hallway. "Whatever you're gonna do, do it fast, Valsaint."

Xavier nodded and ducked into the ruins of the study.

Carlos stood at the bottom of the staircase and peeked around the corner. Kyle was coming up the hallway. The larger boy was rubbing his chin and spitting on the floor as he stumbled toward him. "You're a dead man, Medina! Wait'll I get my hands on you!"

Carlos ascended the stairs until he was about halfway to the second floor. He stopped and looked back down. Kyle had reached the foyer. He looked about, his eyes lingering on the open doorway to the study. He took a step in that direction.

Carlos licked his lips. He was about to do the single dumbest thing he had ever done in his life and he knew it. *Xavier's plan better work,* he thought, and shouted, "Hey, genius, I'm up here!" Kyle whirled. His eyes fixed on Carlos and his lips spread into a hungry grin. Blood dripped from his nose and he sniffled it back. "Time to pay the piper," Kyle said with glee.

"Come and get me." Carlos bolted the rest of the way up the stairs. He chose the hallway on the right, lingering just long enough for Kyle to see which way he went. Then he was running as fast as he could.

*****

Xavier heard Kyle race up the stairs, not even pausing at the collapsed area in his quest for vengeance against Carlos Medina. He hated to turn his friend into a moving target but what he had to do would be difficult enough without Kyle Reed trying to stop him. He just hoped Carlos would be able to stay ahead of the bigger boy long enough for Xavier to follow Caleb's instructions.

Xavier raced down the hallway and into the kitchen. He stopped short when he saw Shawn and Maureen Sullivan. The two siblings knelt on the floor in front of the refrigerator. They were picking up the scattered letter magnets and arranging them into a message on the refrigerator door. They had gotten as far as: FIND TH

Xavier nodded. "The idol, I know."

The two children continued with their task as if he had not spoken, although the little girl favored him with a smile. Xavier smiled back and waved. Then he turned his attention to the basement door.
The last thing in the world he wanted to do was go through that door. Nonetheless he placed his hand on the knob and turned. The door opened easily enough. He peered down the steps and called out, "Andy? You guys down there?"

At first he heard nothing. Then, a soft sobbing. It sounded distant, as if he were listening to the anguish of someone long dead. Xavier swallowed and then took a deep breath. He could not put this off any longer. He thought of Carlos, running around upstairs with an enraged Kyle Reed after him. That more than anything got him moving.

The first step was missing. He stepped over it gently and slowly. The rest of the steps creaked and sagged beneath his weight but they held. He became aware that the temperature seemed to drop more with each step he took into the basement. The bottom step groaned so loudly Xavier's heart almost stopped. *Get a grip*, he told himself. *It's not like you're about to do something incredibly stupid.* Xavier left the steps behind and turned the corner.

The temperature in the basement was polar. Xavier would not have been overly surprised had the place been covered in ice and snow. He took a slow, deep breath, felt the cold air invade his lungs. He shivered, just a little, but enough for anyone watching him to notice.
Andy, Navaeh and Maya knelt in the center of the basement. The sobs he heard were coming from Maya but the other two looked as scared as did she, as scared as Xavier himself. Each child shivered and their teeth chattered. They shook as if they were sitting atop a live electrical wire.

They looked at him with wide, wet, pleading eyes. Xavier took another deep breath. He wanted to say something, say anything that would reassure them. He found he could no longer speak. He merely nodded to them and hoped that would be enough.

The zone of darkness he had first seen erupt from the ground on a Civil War battlefield blocked his view of everything on the far side of his kneeling classmates. Something moved within that darkness. A pair of red eyes blazed at him. A woman's voice seemed to come from all around the basement.

"Come, my child," Tah-tah-Kro'-ah purred. "Join your friends." Xavier inched closer to the darkness. "I know what you are," he said. He paused when he realized his voice had returned. *Better keep going before it disappears on you again*, he thought. *And next time it might not come back at all*. He swallowed again. "You're the raven queen." Tah-tah-Kro'-ah laughed. It was the sound of something heavy being dragged across crushed glass. "Indeed," she replied when the laughter ended.

"Andy, I'm gonna need your help," Xavier said. Andy did not reply. He blinked his wet eyes at Xavier.

Something big moved around from behind the raven queen and stood slightly in front of her, directly behind the three kneeling children. Black Bear's eyes—not quite as brilliant as the woman-thing's— seemed to drill into Xavier's head. Xavier blinked away the slight pain that worked its way into his skull.

His eyes focused on the bear claw that served as the warrior's right hand. Xavier licked his dry lips and took a step back. "I know who you are, too, Black Bear. And I know what you did. Caleb Mason sends his regards."

Black Bear roared as loudly as a real bear. Xavier turned and bolted up the stairs. He could hear the big warrior's heavy footfalls coming after him.

He reached the kitchen and saw the two children were gone. They had stuck around long enough to leave another message. D STROY TH IDOL

"Working on it," Xavier replied to the now-vanished siblings. He slammed the basement door closed just as Black Bear reached the threshold. The door shuddered in its frame and dust drifted down from the ceiling. Xavier heard the Native American warrior grunt and then another impact shook the door. Plaster joined the dust this time. It pattered onto the kitchen floor. Xavier backed up.

The door shattered like glass under the next impact. Rotted wood flew in all directions. Xavier shielded his eyes, felt the splinters sting his hands and his arms. Black Bear entered the kitchen. Xavier turned toward the back door. He stopped dead in his tracks when he saw a pool of what looked like black smoke seep through the cracks in the linoleum and swirl around his feet. The temperature in the kitchen plummeted, raising the gooseflesh on Xavier's arms. The black smoke expanded and rose and became the raven queen. She floated a few inches above the floor, directly in front of Xavier. Her red eyes snapped open.

Xavier could see some of the woman-thing's features. Her mouth was elongated and wide and resembled a bird's beak. *Except no bird has teeth like that*, some part of his mind informed him. Those teeth were long and sharp, more like the fangs of a snake. If she had a nose it was small enough that Xavier could not see it. Her eyes were deeply set and focused squarely on him.

She extended her arms—or maybe they were wings—and wrapped them around Xavier's body. The temperature dropped even more within her embrace and now Xavier's breath frosted the air. "Do not struggle, child," she whispered into his ear. "You will enjoy what I have to show you."

Despite his best efforts tears began to flow from Xavier's eyes. They froze on his skin.

Chapter Fourteen

Xavier Gets Some Fresh Air

"Where you at, Medina? You can't hide from me forever, you know."

Carlos listened with his ear to the door. He guessed Kyle was maybe fifteen feet farther up the hallway, and he was coming closer. One more room to check, maybe two, and Kyle would be on him. It was blind luck Carlos had chosen this room; there was a side door which led to another room. Carlos had opened it and peeked inside and saw what he took to be a sewing room. It gave him a way out if (*when*) Kyle finally found him.

"I give you and Valsaint to the woman, she lets me go," Kyle said. "Where is that little weasel, anyway? He hiding with you?" The sound of a door opening, a pause, then, "I sure hope so. I wanna wrap this up and get home in time for dinner."

Carlos backed away from the door as silently as he could. He tiptoed across the room and stood by the other door. He turned the knob, winced as it produced a squeak. His eyes darted back to where he had been standing.

"Little pigs, little pigs, let me in," Kyle called from the other side of the door. "I heard that, you idiots."

Carlos watched the door handle turn. He was through the other door in an instant. He closed it behind him and looked about. The sewing room contained several mannequins in various states of dress. The ancient fabric which clung to their frames was moth-eaten and covered with dust and cobwebs. A small table still stood near the window. The sewing machine which sat atop the table was old and looked as if it were made of cast iron. The door which led to the hallway stood against the far wall. Carlos started for it.

The floor groaned and buckled beneath his feet. The loud *crack* of wood breaking echoed loudly within the room. Carlos yelped and threw himself back. The floor did not give way but he knew he had come close to going through.

Kyle knocked on the side door. "Stop making this harder than it has to be, Medina."

Carlos scrambled to his feet. He eyed the weak spot in the floor and carefully but quickly made his way around it.

The door flew open and Kyle stepped inside the sewing room. "Hey, Medina. How's it going?" His tone was friendly, even conversational, as if he were seeing an old friend for the first time in years. He slammed his fist into his open palm and glanced about the room. "Valsaint in here somewhere?"

Carlos did not reply. He backed slowly toward the door.

Kyle closed the side door behind him and smiled. "Guess not. That's okay, I'll find him. Or she will."

Carlos put his back to the door.

Kyle advanced on him slowly, his smile still in place. "I'm gonna enjoy the hell out of this."

Kyle's foot found the soft spot on the floor. The wood creaked loudly. With a loud, sharp *crack*, the floor gave way. Kyle yelped and threw his arms out. He managed to catch himself while his upper body was still inside the room. He struggled against the rotting wood but it seemed he was stuck. The uneven, broken edges of the floorboards dug into his skin and tore at his shirt every time he tried to pull himself back up. He cursed and flailed his arms wildly.

"Not as much as I enjoyed that," Carlos finally replied. He opened the door and stepped through.

"We ain't done yet, Medina! As soon as I get outta here you're dead! You hear me? *Dead!*"

"They heard you in Pittsburgh," Carlos said, but he was already back in the hallway and heading for the stairs so Kyle did not hear him.

*****

Xavier's vision started to blur. The edges were growing dark and that darkness was spreading. He struggled against the raven queen's embrace but he was simply not strong enough to break free.

"He is magnificent, isn't he?" she whispered into his ear.

At first he had no idea about whom she was speaking. Then his worsening vision beheld Black Bear. Xavier had actually forgotten his presence. The big warrior made his way slowly across the kitchen in their direction. He raised his giant bear paw. The weakening sunlight from outside glinted off the sharp claws. Xavier closed his eyes.

There was a roar from in front of him. Xavier braced for the impact of those claws on his flesh. Instead he heard a second roar, this one unmistakably from Black Bear. It sounded surprised and angry. Xavier opened one eye and squinted.

Andy clung to Black Bear's back. The boy's left arm was wrapped around Black Bear's neck while his right rained blows on the ancient warrior's bare chest. Black Bear spun about so quickly Andy's legs shot out and he looked, for the briefest of moments, like a trapeze artist in mid-air

"Get the claw! Get the claw!" Xavier shouted.

Andy did not even have time to look at him. Black Bear spun around again and this time Andy lost his grip. He sailed through the air and crashed into the cabinets. The wood splintered and Andy landed on the counter before rolling onto the floor. He groaned but did not move again.

Before Xavier had time to be disappointed it was Nevaeh's turn to leap onto Black Bear's back. Black Bear grunted and flailed at the young girl. That was when Xavier saw Maya take a hesitant step into the kitchen. She was terrified, obviously, and tears streamed freely down her cheeks. Her eyes were focused on her friend and she screamed Nevaeh's name.

It took only a moment for Black Bear to rid himself of the girl. He shrugged his broad shoulders and Nevaeh fell and landed hard on her back. Maya took a single step toward her but froze when Black Bear turned in her direction.

"Leave them alone!" Xavier shouted. Or he might have said nothing. The cold from the raven queen had by now seeped into his bones and his vision was turning black.

"Such spirited little children," Tah-tah-Kro'-ah said. She sounded quite pleased, even proud of them. "Delicious."

Xavier felt himself falling. He landed on the cold kitchen floor and lay there in a heap of quivering muscles. He got the impression the raven queen was moving away from him but he could see nothing. *Sorry, Caleb*, he thought. *I tried.*

*****

Carlos reached the foyer. He heard commotion coming from the kitchen and headed in that direction. As he neared the threshold he stopped and hugged the wall. Shouts. Sounds of things breaking. Grunts that sounded as if they came from a wild animal. He shivered at the sudden drop in temperature. Steeling himself, he inched closer and peered into the kitchen.

It was chaos. Xavier and Nevaeh were down. Maya knelt beside her friend and shook her. Andy lay on the floor near the counter and pushed himself to his knees. The man Xavier described before sending Carlos upstairs loomed above them all. But it was the woman who drew and held Carlos's gaze. Her arms were spread wide as if to encompass the entire room. The darkness around her seemed to form the shape of wings.

Carlos looked again at Xavier. His friend was awake and looked at him with pleading eyes. He said something but it was a croak and Carlos could not hear him. So Xavier pointed at the bird woman. Carlos nodded and looked about frantically. Pieces of broken dishes from the kitchen littered the hallway. He scooped up the biggest piece he could find. Carlos took a deep breath to steady himself. Then he stepped into the doorway and threw the broken dish as hard as he could at the woman.

It vanished into the darkness surrounding her but it must have made contact. She whirled in his direction. Red eyes narrowed as she beheld the small boy in the doorway.

Carlos found himself rooted to the spot. As much as he wanted to turn and run his feet felt as if they had been bolted to the floor. The woman glided across the kitchen in his direction.

That was when Xavier made his move.

✳✳✳✳✳

Xavier willed his muscles to move. Despite the cold, despite the numbness in his limbs, he managed to regain his feet. He needed a moment, just one, to steady himself, but there was no time. With a roar, he threw himself at Black Bear.

The giant warrior was unprepared for such a move. Xavier crashed into him and their momentum carried them toward the back door. Just as Xavier thought they would make it Black Bear bore down and stopped them inches from the target. Xavier's eyes moved up slowly. Black Bear glared at him, his red eyes ablaze with anger. Xavier gulped.

Something heavy crashed into Xavier's back and once again they were moving forward. This time Black Bear could not stop them. They smashed through the back door and suddenly Xavier was outside the house. He landed atop Black Bear but that lasted only a moment. Xavier tumbled off and rolled away. He gulped air; even given his

95

present situation his mind registered how clean and fresh the air smelled. He had not realized until that moment how thick with decay the air inside the house had been. Absently he registered the sudden increase in temperature. It felt sixty degrees warmer outside then it had in the kitchen.

Xavier rolled onto his stomach and pushed himself to his knees. Andy sat atop Black Bear, struggling with the big Indian. *So it was Andy who crashed into us*, Xavier thought. He silently thanked his friend. As Xavier got back on his feet Andy finally lost the battle. Black Bear rolled and wound up on top of the boy. He raised his bear paw. Andy held his arms in front of him and screamed.

Xavier moved.

Chapter Fifteen

Tah-tah-Kro'-ah

Black Bear roared. The giant bear paw descended, its claws slicing the air.

Xavier grasped it with both hands. The sheer strength of the ancient warrior's arm carried Xavier forward and down. His feet left the ground and for a moment he was airborne. Then he slammed onto the hard earth. The breath exploded from his lungs and stars danced across his vision.

He expected to hear Andy scream as those claws cut through him but the scream never came. Xavier rolled onto his stomach and looked at his friend.

Andy was still down, still holding his arms out in front of him to ward off the blow, but it was no longer necessary. Black Bear still knelt atop the boy but there was something different about him. His right arm ended at his elbow. He stared at the stump with genuine astonishment. It was at that moment Xavier realized he had the bear paw in his hands.

Black Bear looked at the empty space that used to be both his limb and his primary weapon. His gaze shifted slowly to Xavier.

Well, I'm about to die, Xavier thought.

Black Bear threw back his head and roared silently into the twilight sky. The wind picked up and whipped through his long hair. His body quivered. As Xavier watched, the ancient warrior's skin turned gray. Flakes fell off and were borne away by the wind. In seconds he was no more than a small dust cloud scattered into the Pennsylvania sky.

Xavier lay on the ground as if frozen to the spot. He may have remained that way if not for the sight of the soldiers marching toward him in rigid military formation. Xavier sprang to his feet and ran for

Andy. The other boy looked about as if he were waking from an inescapable nightmare. His expression became even more horrified when he saw what Xavier held in his hands. He pushed himself away from Xavier and stumbled to his feet. He might have run down the gentle slope of the hill but the sight of the advancing soldiers stopped him in his tracks.

"We have to get back inside," Xavier told him. "Fast!"

Andy looked from the soldiers to the bear paw in Xavier's hands and back to the soldiers.

"Andy! Listen to me! We need to move, *now!*"

The soldiers stopped their advance no more than fifty feet from the two boys. The front row knelt, the back row remained standing. All swung their rifles from their shoulders and aimed them at the two new targets in front of them.

That got Andy moving. He took a single step toward the house. He yelped and clutched his right leg.

Xavier wasted no time. He threw Andy's arm over his shoulder and moved as quickly as the other boy's weight would allow for the broken back door of the house.

No sound came from the soldier's rifles yet Xavier could feel the musket balls whiz past his head. They chewed into the wooden slats of the house and sent plumes of dirt and grass into the air around them. When they reached the steps that led to the back door Xavier threw Andy across the threshold before he hurled himself after the boy. They skidded and rolled across the kitchen floor, coming to rest in front of the refrigerator.

He half-expected to see the soldiers charging into the kitchen through the open door but they had not moved since assuming their firing positions. *Maybe they* can't *come in,* the voice in Xavier's head suggested. *It's not like that old door could have stopped them before.* "Good point," Xavier replied.

His eyes were drawn to the zone of darkness that surrounded Tah-tah Kro'-ah. She hovered above the floor against the far wall of the kitchen. Carlos, Navaeh, and Maya knelt on the ancient linoleum before her. Carlos glanced over his shoulder at Xavier, his eyes pleading.

Xavier grabbed Andy's shoulders. "Try to get away from her. I'm gonna see if I can end this."   Then he dashed for the basement door. He tried to conceal the giant bear paw beneath his shirt as he ran. To his surprise the raven queen did not come after him. *Oh, don't worry, she will*, the voice in his head assured him. *As soon as she's done doing whatever she's gonna do to your friends, you're next on her list*. This time Xavier did not reply.

He took the basement steps two at a time, no longer concerning himself with how they creaked their protest. When he reached the bottom he whirled and started toward the back of the basement. "That's where it has to be, right?" he asked the darkness.

The bear paw grew colder in his hands. The meager light spilling down the steps did not penetrate the far side of the basement and Xavier was quickly enveloped in darkness. "Come on, come on, where is it?"

He gasped suddenly and dropped the bear paw. It had grown so cold it was as if he were holding onto a small slab of ice. Xavier stopped, closed his eyes. It was not just the bear paw that had grown cold; the air temperature around him had plummeted suddenly and dramatically. Xavier opened his eyes and looked down.

There was nothing remarkable about the ground upon which he stood, other than the intense cold radiating from it. Xavier could feel the cold even through the soles of his sneakers. He could see nothing but he knew his breath was frosting the air.

He knelt, felt about the ground. Just as quickly he pulled his hand back. "Geez, that's cold!" He felt about for the bear paw and scooped it up. It was cold but he must be growing accustomed to it; he could tolerate the cold now where he could not a moment before. "This has to be it."

He took a long, slow breath, felt the icy air invade his lungs. This was not going to be fun. Before he could talk himself out of it, he slid his arm into the bear paw. Xavier gasped. The cold within the hollow appendage was deep and penetrated his skin and muscles in an instant. Immediately his arm went numb. The pins-and-needles sensation worked its way up his arm toward his shoulder. "Better hurry," he mumbled.

Xavier raised his arm and swung down with everything he had. The claws tore at the cold, hard ground that made up the basement floor. Frozen dirt pelted his cheeks and his neck. Xavier struck down again.

You'd better proceed with haste, a voice behind him intoned. Xavier did not need to turn to know it was Caleb Mason who spoke. *They're coming.*

"'They're?'" But he was afraid he already knew the answer.

The numbness had reached his shoulder and was continuing its march onward. Already his neck and chest began to stiffen.

On the next swipe at the floor he felt the claws brush something that wasn't dirt. He paused, then whispered, "Found you." He struck the ground again, and again he felt the claws strike something hard and unyielding. Xavier dug furiously, as fast as his numb muscles would allow. Although he could see very little he knew he had succeeded in uncovering something. And he knew what that something was. With his other hand he reached into the hole he had created and withdrew the small black idol from the ground.

If the air around him was cold the idol itself was Arctic. Xavier lost all feeling in his other hand. He yelped and dropped the idol from his numb fingers; it lay on the ground in front of him like a sleeping—but awakening—tarantula.

"Xavier, stop."

This time it was not the ghost of Caleb Mason who spoke. Xavier turned, at once knowing and dreading what he would see. His friends who had accompanied him to the house—and Kyle Reed— stood perhaps ten feet behind him. Their arms were by their sides, their blank eyes stared straight ahead. They could almost have been sleepwalking. And perhaps they were. Behind them, blotting out the light from upstairs, hovered the raven queen.

"She doesn't want to hurt us," Carlos continued. "She only wants to help us to see."

"Listen to her, Xavier," Maya added, her voice and expression as blank as Carlos's.

Xavier gulped. It took every bit of strength he had left to raise the bear claw above his head. He brought it down at the idol.

The raven queen roared and surged past the other kids. Her fingers, tendrils of frigid darkness, wrapped themselves around his wrist. Xavier gasped. The cold which had been slowly overtaking his body now flooded over him and completed the job. The world started to go black around him.

Something pulled down on his arm, a new presence that had not been there a moment before. Xavier opened one eye. Caleb Mason, along with a host of others, the Sullivan children among them, struggled against the force of the raven queen's strength. She screeched her protest at their unexpected resistance.

Caleb looked at Xavier and nodded.

Xavier pulled with everything he had left. Tah-tah-Kro'-ah's black fingers slipped a bit on his wrist. She screeched again and leaned down, her beaklike mouth inches from his face. Her eyes blazed with icy, red fire.

Xavier screamed and brought his arm down with the last of his strength. He slipped from the raven queen's grip and the bear claws raked across the idol. Tah-tah-Kro'-ah threw her head back and wailed. The sound seemed to shake the entire house. Dust drifted down from the ceiling and several ancient knickknacks tumbled from the walls and broke upon the ground.

Again, Caleb told him. He and the other ghosts seemed to be losing their struggle against the raven queen. Xavier could see them starting to fall away.

Xavier did as Caleb told him and struck the idol again. This time the raven queen spread the darkness that was her wings. The spirits flew back and faded from view. Free of them, Tah-tah-Kro'-ah collapsed to the ground. As she did, Xavier's classmates staggered and gripped the walls and each other to keep from falling.

Tah-tah-Kro'-ah pulled herself along the basement floor toward Xavier. Her eyes, ablaze with hatred, focused squarely on him. Her beaklike mouth opened and snapped shut with each inch she gained.

"It's over, Your Highness." Xavier stuck the idol a final time.

The explosion was silent. It threw Xavier into the far corner of the basement. Old junk rained down on him from the walls. He covered up as best as his frozen muscles allowed. Wind tore through the room with such intensity Xavier thought the whole house would collapse upon him.

Yet the house remained standing. The wind, for all its ferocity, died quickly. Xavier became aware that he could hear his own breathing again. The numbness that had overtaken his body vanished all at once. Slowly, afraid of what he might see, he opened his eyes.

Caleb Mason stood over him and favored him with an odd smile. He extended his hand. Xavier took it and Caleb helped him to his feet. *Thank you*, the boy soldier said.

"Don't mention it," Xavier mumbled. Then Caleb was gone and Xavier was left alone in the dark.

No, not alone. He could hear coughs and groans coming from somewhere ahead of him. His arms outstretched, Xavier moved forward. Light began to intrude into the darkness of the basement and Xavier realized he was getting close to the bottom of the steps.

His friends were there, helping each other up and shaking the cobwebs from their minds.

"You guys okay?" Xavier asked.

Maya threw her arms around him and planted a single kiss on his cheek. "Thank you," she whispered.

"Eww!" Andy exclaimed, and laughed.

Navaeh slapped him gently on the back of his head. "Quiet!" She turned to Xavier. "Is that it? Is it over?"

Xavier looked about the mess caused by the silent explosion. "I guess so."

Carlos shook his hand. "Not bad, Valsaint. Of course, *I* did all the heavy lifting." He laughed as well.

There was an audible *thud* from somewhere upstairs. All of them jumped at the sound. Xavier had time to think, *Oh no. She can't be back!* Then he heard Mr. Bisaillon's voice calling from somewhere near the kitchen. "Kids! Kids, are you in here? Are you all right?"

"Down here, Mr. B," Andy called up the stairs. "We're coming up."

Andy led the way up the steps. Kyle Reed held back until he was alone in the basement with Xavier. "Um, you gonna say anything about what I did in here?" He sounded sheepish, a tone Xavier had never heard from Kyle as long as he had known him.

"Probably. Okay, maybe not *all* of it. We'll see." Then he headed upstairs.

Mr. Bisaillon stood in the kitchen. Both girls were hugging him around his waist and both Carlos and Andy stood nearby. All sported broad smiles. Mr. Bisaillon's widened when he saw the last of his missing students emerge from the basement.

"You guys all okay?"

"More or less," Xavier replied. "How'd you get away from those soldiers?"

Mr. Bisaillon shrugged. "They just wandered off a few minutes ago. Never said a word the whole time. The ravens, too. Flew away in all directions. As soon as they left I came inside. The front door was so rotted it fell inside the house as soon as I touched it." He looked about the ruined kitchen. "What the heck happened in here?"

"It's a long story," Carlos told him.

"You got that right," Navaeh added.

"I'm just glad you guys are okay," Mr. Bisaillon told them. "Oh, Xavier, I found something that belongs to you." He reached into his back pocket and withdrew Xavier's cell phone.

Xavier gaped. "I forgot all about this!" He powered it up and was rewarded with three solid bars at the top of the display. "I think it's gonna work!" He called up his home number and hit the green button.

At first he heard nothing. For an awful moment he thought the raven queen had returned, her disappearance a cruel trick to play upon the kids before she took them all away. He even took a step toward the kitchen door, ready to run straight through it if that's what it took to get out of the house. He looked into the eyes of everyone in the kitchen. They stared back at him. No one breathed.

Then he heard the familiar ringtone and after a moment, his mother's voice. "Xavier? Xavier, where are you?"

He released a breath he was unaware he held and smiled broadly. His companions started breathing again. Carlos and Andy slapped each other's hands.

"Mom, there's no way you're gonna believe me, so here's Mr. Bisaillon. He'll explain the whole thing."

"Honey, wait! What—"

Xavier offered the phone to his teacher. Mr. Bisaillon ruffled Xavier's hair and took the phone. As he began to speak to the woman on the other end, Xavier looked at his friends.

"Let's get the hell outta here."

Amid nods of agreement and some relieved laughter, they headed for the front door.

J. C. Logan

Joe grew up in Connecticut's Naugatuck Valley. A voracious reader since he was old enough to hold a book in his hands, he surprised his second-grade teacher by using the word "invulnerable" (learned from a Superman comic book) in a sentence. He wrote his first story at the ripe old age of 11. His published works include the novels *The Last Battleship* and *Moon Dust*. His favorite authors and influences include Richard Matheson, Rod Sterling, Agatha Christie, Stephen King, Alan Moore and Neil Gaiman.

The Gibbeting

Elizabeth Alsobrooks

A shrill scream sounded in the mist.

Rachel faltered, lost focus and tripped over a root. The ground rushed at her so fast she didn't have time to catch her breath before it slammed out of her chest. *Get a grip or you're gonna die. Concentrate on pushing the air out. That's it. Now slowly, slowly, draw breath back into your lungs. Okay. Again. Willing herself to relax, she took another breath before forcing herself to her knees and then her feet.*

Eyes narrowed in order to search the foggy dusk behind her, she listened intently for a faint footfall or soft moan. If only she could reach Mike's house. It had to be close now. Satisfied she'd outdistanced her pursuer she turned and again ran toward the clearing she knew to be ahead. *Less than the distance down Viejo Sabio's main street now. Almost there. I'm almost there. I can make it.*

I have to make it.

There, Jaws is barking. He must hear me coming. I'm close.

The mastiff's howling grew louder and more determined until she at last raced out of the small wash that bordered Mike's house, her feet crunching on the pebble stone-scaping in his back yard. "It's me, it's just me, Jaws. Calm down." A quick gasp and she clutched at her side and pushed herself forward, down the side of the adobe dwelling, careful to skirt the large pear cactus. Around the front she pounded on the thick mesquite door, vaguely noting that Jaws had been barking toward the house, not the field behind it from which she'd just come.

She backed up to see if any lights shone through the glass, tripped over a jack-o-lantern and swore, kicking it aside. The trick-or-treaters had been in bed for hours.

The heavy door inched forward in response to her more frantic assault. She stopped hammering on it with her fists. *Why is that door unlocked in the middle of the night?*

Clomp. Shuffle. Clomp. Shuffle. Up the road a bit. *Is that boots on asphalt? Sounds like something is being dragged. A lame foot perhaps?*

The doorknob felt cold, too cold. A quick push allowed her to slide inside. She slammed it shut behind her and slid the bolt home. *Something's wrong here, but I am certain of what's out there, headed this way. I'll take my chances here at Mike's.*

"Mike? Judge Yazzie?"

The house remained silent. The front room looked empty from what she could tell by the soft glow of the last dying embers in the fireplace. *They're probably asleep. So why the open door? Is someone else in here too? Something else?* Hands fisted to steel her nerves she paused a moment to catch her breath. The sweet pungent aroma of burned mesquite wafted toward her from the hearth.

"Mike? Hello. It's me, Rachel. Is anyone home?"

Ten stairs later, she knocked on her fiancé's bedroom door and didn't wait for an answer before she burst inside. "Mike! Wake up!"

"Rachel?" He rubbed his eyes as he sat up, his brows creased in confusion and concern. "What the hell are you doing here? What time is it?" He stood and reached for his jeans. "What's wrong?"

"You won't believe it. I don't believe it. I can't believe it."

A zip and a button later, he scuffed his feet into slippers and placed his hands on her shoulders. "Okay. Calm down, honey. Take a breath and tell me what you're doing here," he glanced out the window, then down at the clock on his nightstand, "in the middle of the night. Hey, you're shaking."

"Frank Locklear just killed by roommate, Star."

He took a step back to better examine her face. "Frank? The Sabio Strangler Frank?"

She nodded. "And I think he followed me h—"

The crash and shouting drew both their attention toward the door. "What the hell was that?" Mike put out his arm to edge around her, or more probably to push her behind him, before running through the doorway and across the hall to his grandfather's bedroom.

Rachel already suspected who or what was there. She bent to reach under his bed and grab his double barrel. Check. Loaded. Pump. Already set to fire.

"What the fuck!" Crash. "Fuck you!"

She ran toward the commotion. The door was open, but it was dark. A lamp lay on its side near the doorway. Movement near the window. She could make out shapes against the faint distant glow of the streetlight. Two men struggled, a fight to the death . . . or beyond. She knew one was Mike. *Which one?* The gun barrel tracked one shadowed silhouette, then the other.

Reaching and feeling along the wall, she connected with the switch. The ceiling light illuminated the combatants. Mike was closest, in the way of a good shot. "Mike, get over here. I've got the rifle."

He glanced her way, shoving against not a man but a very tall and stocky woman, Mary Jones.

The first blast went right but Rachel's adrenaline helped her adjust to the recoil and the second hit Mary in the face as she rushed forward to attack Mike. The force jerked her head backward as it carried her brain matter to the window, where it splattered against the panes. Rachel had little time to contemplate it before the momentum conducted Mary into the glass where she crashed outward and down amidst the bloodied shards.

Rachel didn't care to investigate Mary's landing, so she scanned the room. *There.* Judge Yazzie lay crumpled on the floor in the corner. She raced across the room and knelt down. Mike reached for the heavy D12 double barrel and she gently tugged on Judge Yazzie's shoulder until he rolled over. Unconscious, but his chest rose and fell. *Alive. Thank God.* "Judge Yazzie, can you hear me? Judge, wake up."

He groaned in response.

"Gramps. Gramps, it's me, Mike." He stooped beside her and ran his hand down his grandfather's chest, and then his extremities.

"Check his head. Maybe he got knocked out."

Mike set the gun down and gently lifted his grandfather's head, probing for a wound. "Yup, an egg right here on the back of his noggin."

"Where's your cell? I'll call 911."

"Nightstand."

Rachel hurried back across the hall and snatched the phone, entering the triple digits on her way back. In such a small town, the solitary operator answered almost immediately. "Francis, we need the police and paramedics over here at Mike's house. An intruder attacked the judge. Yes. No, they're, um, shot."

The front door smashed into the wall. Rachel jumped and dropped the phone. She hurried to the rail and looked down into the foyer. *No. It can't be.* "Mike! Get out here! Bring the rifle!"

He charged into the hallway and looked down. "What the hell is going on, Rachel?"

Rachel's heart pounded so hard her ears rang. *What appears to be happening can't be possible. It just can't.* Just when her adrenaline level started to dissipate Mary's headless body stumbled into the house, somehow, sightlessly, finding the first stair.

"Jesus, Mary and Joseph."

Then, just behind Mary, Frank staggered inside. *He found me.* "You're gonna need all the saints too, to get us outta this one, Mike."

Mike's eyes were wide and glassy with shock and disbelief. "Both murderers, and both dead," he said softly. "They're dead, right Rachel? They have to be dead by now."

And so they should be. The Sabio Strangler, as Frank had been dubbed by some reporter down at the local newspaper, had raped and strangled six women, that they knew of, though he claimed it was more. And Mary, she'd drowned both her children in the bathtub when her husband ran off with the mail carrier. They and two other criminals were tried, found guilty by a jury of their peers, and sentenced, by Mike's gramp.

Their sentence was handed down in the manner their people had been meting out justice for hundreds of years. Gibbeting. But their small community descended from Puebloans, and they didn't hang their capital crime criminals from a tree. They staked them spread-eagle in the middle of the desert, a clearing said to be so cursed with the restless spirits of the damned that not even cactus grew there.

The gibbeted criminals died of dehydration before starvation, within days, sometimes even before they were eaten by wolves, coyotes or other desert animals. It had been over a week of unusual, for this time of year, blistering heat-filled days and chill nights, surrounded by animals that hadn't seen the relief of a rainfall in months.

"Yes, of course they're dead."

Mary didn't move as quickly without her head. She reached the third step just as Frank reached the second.

Rachel jumped again when the gun sounded. Mary flew backward into Frank. They both landed at the foot of the stairs.

Footfalls pounded up the front steps and two uniformed officers entered in time to see partial Mary and angry Frank struggling to their feet. The policemen stopped in their tracks and the paramedics directly behind them nearly collided.

"Frank killed Star and Mary tried to kill the judge. He's hurt and upstairs."

As if galvanized by her statements, the sheriff and his deputy hurried forward to . . . arrest, or somehow apprehend the killers. They managed to subdue Mary with zip ties around her ankles and wrists, but Frank was another battle. The two of them, and then the two paramedics, and then Rachel armed with a ball bat and Mike with his rifle beat him to the ground. Once there, still fighting like a wild animal, complete with growls and bared teeth, Frank finally slowed enough to be handcuffed after the Sheriff shot him in the forehead.

It was then that Rachel noticed the rancid stench. She wrinkled her nose and stepped aside to let the paramedics hurry up the stairs.

"Which room?" one of them asked.

Mike gave them directions and rushed after them.

A moment later Rachel felt relieved to hear the judge talking, but she was still unable to tear her eyes off the two struggling corpses in a pool of blood and gore at her feet. "What if all the criminals ever gibbeted there have reanimated to seek their revenge?"

"What's that you're saying?" Sheriff Gillis asked.

"They're dead. They have to be dead, but they're not leaving. Their vengeful souls are still here, and they want revenge. I know it sounds crazy, but what other explanation is there?"

"How the hell could this have happened and what can we do about it now?" The deputy fired another round into Frank who seemed determined to rise.

Two more policemen arrived, the entire force now, and after their initial shock and disbelief, helped the sheriff and the other deputy remove the corpses, despite their continued struggling.

The sheriff reappeared long enough to ask Rachel where her roommate's body was located, advising her to stay available for an interview and hurried off to take his prisoners away.

The judge, head wrapped with white gauze, Mike and the paramedics emerged from bedroom and despite his refusal to use the gurney, the judge did accept help maneuvering the stairs.

"Mike, I don't need you coddling me. The paramedics will see that I'm looked after. Take Rachel and go see the medicine man. See what must be done." When Mike tried to protest, his grandfather took on the demeaner that made criminals quake and said, "do it now, young man."

Mike nodded as his grandfather left under the care of the medics and reached for his boots standing beside the front door. Once he'd kicked off his slippers and pushed his feet into them, he grabbed his keys off the hook. "Coming?"

"So ordered by the judge."

He nodded again, reached to switch on the porch light and then walked outside and waited for her to exit before locking the front door. She raised her brow and he shrugged, glancing at the remaining police car where Deputy Sanders argued, "I'm not getting into this vehicle with that thing in the back. What if it's a zombie and it bites me?"

"Get in the car you moron," the sheriff said. "She's in the cage. Now get the hell in the car."

The she in question began clawing and banging on the window, her headless torso writhing in frustrated rage, leaving an unpleasant smear of body fluids on the glass.

"But Sheriff—"

"She doesn't have a head, and that means no teeth. How's she gonna bite you?"

"Said no one ever," Mike pointed out as he headed to the garage for his old classic, a refurbished Chevelle SS. He stowed his shotgun in the back seat and reached to take his grandfather's, the one Rachel grabbed from above the fireplace on the way out.

It took less than five minutes to get to the medicine man's house, just a few blocks away. He was standing in the doorway when they pulled into his driveway. Neither of them felt surprised. It was the least odd thing that had happened tonight.

"Come in," Golden Eagle said. "I've been preparing."

They didn't ask for what. They knew what.

"Here, take this and put it in the back of my pickup." He handed Mike a gas can and an actual torch. Though it wasn't lit, the soaked cloth and saran wrapped pole reeked of something petroleum based, something flammable. He handed two more to Rachel.

"Why do you suppose he doesn't just use flashlights?" Rachel carefully laid the torches in the bed of the old Chevy.

"No idea. Tonight, I'm just taking things as they come." He paused to turn and look at her. "How are you holding up? I haven't had a chance to say how sorry I am about Star, and I know you've not had time to deal with your grief yet."

She threw her arms around him and buried her face against his familiar chest for a moment, taking in the fresh soap smell that lingered from the shower he must have taken before bed. "Thank you, babe. You're always so calm, even in situations like . . . like this. I just kept telling myself that everything would be okay if only I could reach you."

"And it will be," he said, lifting her chin to press a quick kiss to her lips. "Now that you found me, so you can help keep me safe." His welcome smile flashed for a moment. "Come on, let's grab the rifles and see if Golden Eagle needs anything else. I have an uncomfortable feeling I know where he's going to take us."

Rachel nodded. *Yeah, I know too.*

A few moments later, they were headed away from town, Rachel snugged in between Golden Eagle and Mike. Glad for the warmth, she wondered if she'd ever be warm again, even in the desert. Tonight's events chilled her to her bones. Rubbing her hands across her knees, she noted that they no longer shook.

"So are all the legends we used to tell each other as kids true, Golden Eagle?"

The elder glanced toward Rachel, then focused his attention to the road as he turned the Chevy onto a rough unmarked road. She noticed

Mike trying to catch her eye and nodded. They both knew their destination.

"Most all legends are founded on truths. Ours probably more so than others. They were stories handed down through the generations by the elders in order to help our people learn from the mistakes of the past. The medicine men handed down truths most are better off not knowing until the time has come."

"And has it? Has the time come, Golden Eagle?"

"Yes, Michael, the time has come." With that, he parked the truck and opened his door. As she exited, Rachel noticed for the first time that Golden Eagle was not only wearing his usual buckskins, he was wearing sacred ceremonial apparel. He reached into the bed and grabbed a torch, quickly unwinding the cellophane and tossing it back. Pulling a lighter out of his pocket, he flicked it. "Unwrap them."

Rachel and Mike tossed the wraps then held them out, catching fire from the first.

"One of you needs to grab that gas," he instructed as he reached for his duffle and flung it over his shoulder.

Mike slung the strap on his rifle over his shoulder and grabbed the can with his free hand. "Maybe we're going to light a bonfire."

Rachel shrugged and headed after Golden Eagle. What she saw when she got to the clearing shocked her as much as anything else she'd seen that night. A chill snaked its way up her spine, leaving her paralyzed.

"Damn."

More likely damned.

Most years there were none. In fact it must have been at least a decade since the last. This year they had four. An unusually high number as gibbeting went in the village of Viejo Sabio. It was a brutal punishment reserved for the perpetrators of truly heinous crimes, crimes for which there could be no redemption.

Frank should have been killed years ago, but they hadn't discovered who the serial rapist/strangler in their midst was until this year. Mary, well, taking her anger at her husband out on her innocent children was about as unforgiveable as it got.

Which was why Jacob was there. After a decade of severe abuse, he had finally killed his wife, and she'd been carrying their sixth child at the time. Her parents had gladly taken her children home to live with them. No one thought Jacob a fit father, or human being, for that matter.

Finally, and most surprisingly to Rachel, there was Sammy, the brother of Emily, who everyone believed to be the town slut, with three illegitimate children whose father she refused to name. Until one of them told his teacher what his uncle was doing to his terrified mother and little sister and the town discovered Sammy was their father as well as their uncle. He'd been raping his little sister since she was eight and molesting his own daughter since she was six.

Rachel had been friends with Emily in fourth grade, and now understood why the girl had grown so aloof and unkempt. She'd tried to reconnect, but the still frightened woman remained distant and secluded.

But there lay the bastard who'd ruined Emily's life for so many years. Still tied to the four stakes that had been driven so far into the stone and sand he never could have escaped. And yet, Frank and Mary were on a rampage, and their weather and animal ravaged remains still lay where they'd been left.

"How is it possible? Are they ghosts?"

"The evil in their souls lives on." Golden Eagle dropped his bag onto the ground and stuck his torch into a nearby stand. He then reached into the bag and began pulling out items he needed for a ceremony. "I told the Judge not to let them carry out the sentencing until after the full moon. Sheriff wanted to string out Sammy as soon as possible. Never seen the man so worked up. Seems like I recall him having a crush on Emily when they were youngsters."

"Are you saying their souls are walking the earth and . . . killing people? How is that possible?"

"Not their souls. The evil manifested within them and within all those who have died before them. It has grown until it's powerful enough, on this Day of the Dead, to be reborn."

"You're kidding? How are we supposed to stop some evil entity?"

"Pour gas on all four bodies, Michael."

"What?"

"Now, son."

Mike glanced at Rachel, shaking his head. Then, he moved to what little remained of Sammy, a pile of torn and ragged clothing, bones and a portion of his head. The eyes and brains would have been first to go. What the birds didn't get the ants would. He uplifted the gas can and poured fuel from head to toes and moved on to Frank's remains.

"What can I do to help?"

"Lay out the offerings from the bag," Golden Eagle said sliding his fingers along his cheekbone as he applied colorful streaks of paint. Wiping his hands on a rag, he stood and pulled on his headdress. "Hand me those rattles."

Rachel reached over to drop her torch into another holder of the five that formed a small circle in the center of the clearing. She rummaged in the bag and found the set of gourds and handed them to the medicine man. Then she pulled out what she recognized to be representative of the three remaining elements, a jar of earth from the top of the sacred mountain, a paper kite in the shape of an eagle, to be lit by the fire already in use and let loose on the wind, and a bottle of holy water complete with a small cross etched into the glass. *Some things have changed.*

"Put them in the center."

She walked to the middle of the clearing and deposited the offerings. Mike finished his assignment and the scent of burning hair and gasoline surrounded them. She rubbed her hand across her nose.

"Light it."

Rachel knew what he wanted. She walked toward Mike, unfolding the small kite and extending it so he could torch it, too. Then she swung it skyward where the brisk night breeze caught and carried it higher.

The sound of the crackling fires mingled with Golden Eagle's chanting and rhythmic rattling as he danced around the circle, performing an ancient cleansing ceremony in the language of their forefathers. He held both gourds in one hand and reached into the bag. Then, dancing in circles, he approached the flaming remains of what had once been Sammy, flinging a handful of something that sparked and sizzled as the fire ignited it.

His chanting increased.

Both Rachel and Mike watched Golden Eagle's ceremony with reverent fascination. They might have stepped back in time hundreds of years to the original pueblo. Rachel swayed in time with the medicine man's hypnotic rhythm. He was in a meditative trance, calling upon his spirit guides and the Tiwa tribe's ancestors to aid him in sending the evil entities back to the dark realm.

"Aaargh!"

Mike stumbled forward, trying to catch his balance.

Rachel realized what attacked him. She spun around and lifted her rifle, aiming it at Sammy's snarling face. The recoil jerked into her right shoulder, but she held firm, pumped and preparing to shoot again. Sammy, grazed but by no means incapacitated, lurched ahead.

Golden Eagle increased his movements and then stooped to grab another handful of whatever herbal magic he'd concocted. He danced in a wide arc, tossing the mystery dusting across the remaining corpses.

Mike backed away from the approaching madman and raised his double barrel. Already pumped, he pulled the trigger and the right barrel struck Sammy in the chest. He staggered backward, shook his head and kept coming.

Mike's second round hit Sammy in the left arm. It jerked him around and Rachel's hit him in the side of the head. He finally went down, allowing Rachel and Mike to glance over at Golden Eagle.

Before him the corpse of Jacob writhed and groaned, and then screamed, a hideous gut-wrenching sound. Dark mist swirled around him. Golden Eagle chanted in earnest, head down, rattles and the feathers of his headdress shaking. He lifted one foot, stomp, hop, the other foot, stomp, hop, spin, spin, stomp, his song rising in volume with the increase in his movement.

Rachel tilted her head. She smelled something pungent and sweet, something wafting across the clearing on the night breeze. The medicine man's magic.

It was working.

She heard his voice joined by others, by the ancestors. She jumped as a bright swirling cloud of light passed her and descended on the writhing body of Sammy. The shifting mass resembled an eagle in flight, wings spread and flapping over the dark shape that now replaced what once looked to be Sammy but now appeared to be a dark humanoid shadow with red glowing eyes. The ethereal mists struggled for domination, each trying to extinguish the other.

Soon, there were others, encircling the clearing in faster and smaller orbits. Up, down, swirling, rushing from one burning pyre to the next. The space became illuminated with massing entities, one resembling a bear, another a wolf.

The velocity of the wind they created pushed Rachel and Mike backward. They clung to one another and lowered their heads against the storm-like atmosphere. All four fires whipped down, nearly out, then rushed upward, transformed into black silhouettes intent on distinguishing the light. The backdraft sucked the entire contents of the pyres up and they too swirled and writhed,

"What the hell?" Mike yelled to be heard above the din of the wind, the chanting, the rattles.

"I know, but it looks like it's working."

A column of white fragrant smoke spun itself into a tornado and the sound grew deafening.

"Look out!" Rachel squeezed Mike's hand and tugged.

They turned and ran, putting distance between themselves and the cone of the tornado forming in the center of the clearing. Feeling enough distance passed to be safe, they looked back in time to see the glowing cloud swallow what remained of the dark, evil entities. It then shot straight upward and vanished, throwing the space into darkness.

Only one torch still flickered in the cold night breeze. It cast enough light for Rachel to make out the shape of Golden Eagle, collapsed to his knees, nearby. She ran forward and leaned down, putting her arm around him.

"Are you alright?"

He nodded. "Need water."

"Mike, I saw a bottle in the duffle."

Golden Eagle set down the rattles and pulled off his headdress. He pushed his hand across his forehead and into his hairline, wiping at the perspiration. Though not as long as Mike or Rachel's, and no longer glistening black, Golden Eagle's grey hair fell past his shoulders and even in the dim light cast by the nearby torch it looked damp.

The medicine man would recover from his ordeal, but none of them would ever forget the way he valiantly battled the evil forces that night.

Mike handed Rachel a water, and she twisted the cap and placed the bottle in Golden Eagle's hand. He swallowed half its contents in one go before panting softly to catch his breath.

They all turned at the sound of sirens. Flashing emergency lights appeared on the dirt road behind them.

Soon, Sheriff Gillis and Deputy Sanders ran toward them.

"I knew you'd be here. What happened?"

"He cleansed the place of the evil gathering here," Mike said. "What happened to your prisoners?"

"Vanished. Gone, just disappeared right in front of us."

"Yeah," the deputy added. "They were thrashing around, tearing up the cots and stuff in the cells and then suddenly poof, vanished."

"Thanks to Golden Eagle."

"And to the ancestors," Golden Eagle reminded them.

"You're going to have to start sending prisoners to the state for punishment, Sheriff. Some traditions are best left in the past."

No one responded. She knew they were thinking over what she'd said. Rachel stood and helped Mike pull Golden Eagle to his feet. He leaned against the younger man as he finished the water.

"Nature can no longer sustain such destructive negativity. We must take better care of what the great spirit has given us."

Mike had to have his shoulder put back into its socket properly and Rachel had a few stitches in her arm, They were bruised and sore for a week, and both still had occasional nightmares.

Rachel attended the funeral of her roommate Star, feeling sad over her new friend's passing. One other body, discovered by her daughter, was found. Helena Hunter. That one of the evil beings killed her was obvious, but which one probably didn't matter. Most agreed they were lucky to have been spared more deaths that night.

A few weeks later, Mike told Rachel the medicine man returned with the priest and some of the elders. They thoroughly cleansed and blessed the clearing, and already there were a few cactus and wildflowers growing where once only the remains of the wicked resided.

Perhaps, she decided, they should hold their wedding ceremony there.

Elizabeth Alsobrooks

Elizabeth lives with her personal social media editor, Hudson (AKA Maltese), and husband, Kenton, (AKA Irish-Scotsman) at the foot of the beautiful Santa Catalina Mountain Range in AZ. She loves to sit on her patio sipping coffee (or wine) and reading, editing, or brainstorming plots and enjoys the grandeur of her mountain views.

These days, she divides her writing time between urban fantasy, horror, and nonfiction. Work on her Illuminati series continues, but she loves throwing out a horror short on occasion. She grew up with a love for Shakespeare, Chaucer, Poe, Dickens, the Bronte sisters and Koontz, so her taste is as eclectic as her range. That creativity also expresses itself in her oil painting and sculpting.

Death Visits Once A Year

Francesca Quarto

Mist shrouded my face as it blew in from the restless seas below. Sunset was but a few hours off. I urged the borrowed hag to pull the creaky wagon onto the rough track leading into the village of Bountiful.

Tucked into a remote area overlooking the English coastline, its inhabitants were hermit-like in their seclusion even in this modern day of 1881. Nevertheless, in neighboring hamlets, tales of evil doings by Bountiful's Druid descendants held on tenaciously, like barnacles to a ship.

As a reporter at the Daily Voice, I planned to investigate rumors of supernatural occurrences and unnatural ceremonies held by the residents of Bountiful each All Hallows Eve, which was this very night. As subterfuge, I dressed the part of an itinerant peddler.

When the village commons came into view, I allowed my horse to pick his way over the deep ruts, permitting me time to look around.

The village buzzed with activity. The commons, with its scattered shops, was being decorated by several comely women. None took note of my passing, even though my wagon rattled as it rolled by. Oddly, I saw no menfolk about.

The sun shifted toward twilight as I drove on.

I gazed wide-eyed at macabre displays of ghoulish spirits, devouring life-like human limbs. Bundles of straw had been placed beneath blazing torches. Their buttery light illuminated terrifying figures stuffed with rags, sitting below. These looked disturbingly like lunatics from Bedlam's deepest cells.

I couldn't repress a shudder while passing one hairy creature resembling a fabled werewolf, gnawing on a dangling victim.

This is a desolate place, I reflected, when someone jumped directly into the path of my horse, causing it to rear-up in panic. I had to pull on the reins with all my strength to stop the beast from trampling the fool into the dirt. Keeping my seat, trying to gather my wits, the most enchanting girl stepped to my side.

"I fear I've upset yer dray and caused ye some discomfort as well."

I looked down upon the face of an ethereal beauty, and felt myself being pulled into the depths of her sea-green eyes.

"I be Casandra. Ye are welcomed to Bountiful on All Hollow's Eve. Have ye traveled a long distance, then?"

I composed myself, saying I traveled the countryside selling my elixirs. When I finished this pale explanation, I noted a small smile playing on her lush mouth.

"Ye must bring yer wagon and horse to the Blacksmith's to board, until after we have enjoyed our celebration, else, ye shall have none to show yer wares."

Following her directions like a fawning pupil, I drove the horse and wagon to the barn, adjacent to the Smithy's. Placing a nosebag on him, I gave him a good rub-down as he ground his feed.

I returned to the square, surprised to find it empty of town folk. Looking about, I wandered over to a low-roofed shop across the way. A sign hanging above the door swayed in the salty breeze. It read Heart's Blood Inn in poorly printed red lettering, mostly washed-out to a pinkish hue thanks to the workings of the seaside elements.

I peered through a pane-less window. Lit candles revealed a handful of wooden tables, chairs and a rough, plank bar. Having nothing to eat since dawn, I hoped to find a suitable supper within.

No Innkeeper greeted me upon entering. I hallooed, to make my presence known, seating myself at a table as I waited to be noticed. Cobwebs hung like bunting off low, wood-beams. Gritty dust covered every surface and piled into corners. The place had the look of abandonment. I was about to leave when the rich aroma of cooking meat wafted tantalizingly around my head. My mouth immediately watered at the prospect of roast with potatoes and thick gravy. I stepped to the curtain hanging between the bar and what I believed was likely a small kitchen.

Peeking in, I spied a circle of village women, all wearing colorful gowns, showing a daring amount of creamy skin. They sat around an enormous black pot, boiling over a hot fire-pit. Bubbles burst on the iron sides, releasing a pungent, meaty aroma.

"Too soon!" one woman shouted. "We must wait upon the Vampyre afore we can act!" another beauty said. Still another added, "Casandra is preparing. Be patient, sisters! She has already taken measure of the stranger." "Aye," said another, of the six I counted. "And she finds him delicious looking in all respects!"

The comment brought them all to hysterical laughter, throwing their heads back and braying like donkeys. The ungodly sound raised the hair on my neck. In the confines of the heated room, their combined breaths overwhelmed even the smell rising from the pot. I nearly gagged, as I quickly withdrew my head from around the curtain.

My hunger forgotten, I felt stunned at what I'd overheard.

They called Casandra a Vampyre! Were they merely suggesting at yet another Celtic fable, like the mystical power of the Yew Tree?

Not chancing discovery, I made straight for the Blacksmith's. I needed to hitch the horse back to the wagon. Getting a story about Bountiful had become less-important than getting out of it.

Passing through the Blacksmith's shop, I decided I needed a weapon. I found a small hatchet, newly honed, among his Farrier equipment. Grabbing it, I felt relieved having a means of defense, although I knew not what I would be fighting. I slipped it into my belt, taking a measure of comfort as it pressed against my back.

I rushed into the adjacent barn, only to discover an empty stall. The old Dray's feedbag lay half-full on the ground, but there was no sign of the horse. As I stood there, bewildered by the horse's disappearance, the fragrant smell of a hearty meat stew, floated through the open barn door and I knew. "They're cooking my horse!"

I rushed outside, looking frantically in both directions. I needed to escape this crazed village, where the handsome females would eat a visitor's stead! I ran through the square, filled with purple-black shades hiding from a setting sun. Strung wild flowers, some thorny and foul, hung across the roadway,slapping menacingly at my face, while paper bats whizzed by my ears. I moved like a hare, a hungry fox on its tail, until I passed the last bale on the edge of the village. Its hideous werewolf mannequin seemed to stir on his seat as I fled past.

Relieved to have reached the outskirts of Bountiful, I slowed my pace, clutching at my side, burning as it was with a stich of pain. I needed to rest before I collapsed from exertion.

The scudding clouds moved off, revealing a full moon. I spied a hay block in the distance and made for it. Figuring I was far enough away from Bountiful to be safe from discovery, I plopped down with a relieved sigh. I felt drained and longed for my hard seat on the wagon, behind my sturdy dray. The cool breeze pressed my sweaty shirt to my chest, bringing on a shiver.

My breathing had become less-ragged, until a strong hand gripped my shoulder. I jumped to my feet, spinning around and shrieking with fright. The beautiful Casandra looked back at me.

She now wore the same revealing gown as the six women cooking my horse. Her hair was loose, blowing suggestively across her pale bosom. Her eyes fastened on mine and I inexplicably moved closer. Her smile broadened, pulling her full, red lips back. The bright moonlight bathed her lovely face and I saw the gleam of long incisors. I was transfixed by her eyes, barely conscious of what this meant.

She reached up, wrapping a stone-cold hand around my head, drawing me closer. Gently grabbing a fist-full of my hair, she pulled my head back. I saw her lean forward and felt her chilly breath on my neck.

Suddenly, a huge figure burst from the shadows. In a blur, it rammed into her, taking them both to the ground.

I was rooted in place, while Casandra and the very real werewolf tore into each other. Somehow rousing myself, I took flight down the road. I kept running until the grunts and yowls from the two monsters faded into the deep silence.

Without cart, nor horse, I was faced with long hours of trekking back to London by foot. Still pulsing inside from sudden flight, my pace barely slackened. Watching the moon traveling its own path, I figured I'd been nearly two hours of crashing through the wilds. I began to feel light-headed. Finding myself near a field of unharvested corn, I chopped off an ear with the small hatchet, gnawing the kernels like a squirrel.

I just cut off a second ear when the tall stalks in front of me began to shake and sway. Someone was moving through them, coming directly toward me. I lowered the hand holding the hatchet, waiting.

Long, pale fingers pulled the nearest shafts to the side and out stepped the lovely Casandra. "Why'd ye leave, afore the festivities began? Our village only enjoys this celebration once in a year. We mayn't disappoint them."

My voice trembled, but I had to know. "Are you...are you truly a Vampyre as I heard the women name you?"

Her brittle laughter ripped through my ears like shards of glass before she answered.

"Indeed, ye find me so. The Coven of beauties ye spied upon, were pledged in service to me, many centuries past. In exchange, I keep them fair and fed. Each All Hallows' Eve, we must renew our unique bond. There are always the curious like yerself, to help us bring it off."

Her coy giggle unnerved me.

I stammered something about the wolf-creature when the tall stalks rattled again.

The six women who made stew of my horse stepped out from between the rows. The moonlight clearly showed blood and matter spattered over clothes and bare flesh alike. As they grinned, sharp teeth glinted like daggers and I knew these were surely Witches!

Casandra stepped closer, taking the cob from my stiff fingers.

"Let us return now, to the village. The tussle with the lycanthrope, made me near ravenous and I can hear yer heart pumping deliciously!"

"What happened to...it?" I croaked, still unable to move.

"Why, the girl's made a treat of him, after I tricked him to revert. Let me think.

 He was that country doctor, right, Jeannette?"

A dark headed girl nodded, licking between her fingers at some oozing matter.

Her action was like an electric jolt. With one fluid motion, I brought up the small hatchet and swinging in a wide arc, connected with Casandra's slim neck.

Her head lopped clean off, rolling on the ground and coming to rest among the corn stalks.

The six women rushed to the gory spot, sending hair-raising howls into the night.

I knew the she-devils would tear me to pieces and was galvanized to flee.

"I was fortunate when a fruit wagon stopped on the road into London. I came directly here to file my story while it's still fresh, Sir."

The editor held the sheaf of papers in his hands, looking over his glasses at me and shook his head.

"Sorry, son. Too late to run anything about All Hallows Eve shenanigans. Got more important things to cover like the disappearance of a country doctor. His last call was supposed to be an out-of-the-way village. Named, Bountiful, I think. Want to cover that?"

Francesca Quarto

Francesca has worked in local television, a small city zoo, founded a non-profit tutoring agency for an inner-city neighborhood which eventually served local school districts, worked for an International Evangelical Television and Radio Station and for a non-profit organization serving challenged adults.

Francesca Quarto resides in a small town outside of Indianapolis, Indiana with her husband Patrick. She still has a great love of the written word and while she enjoys her E-Reader immensely, she still treasures the excitement of turning the next page.

You Can Never Leave

Ric Wasley

The tinny blast of an air horn hit me like a physical blow. My nodding head jerked upright and I got my first hint that I wasn't going to make LA tonight. Out of the inky black of the two-lane desert highway a speeding semi inexplicably appeared in my lane.

Oops. Revise that. Actually, he was not in my lane - I was in his. I dozed off and wandered across the center line directly into the path of a big brown UPS truck. I would have given the driver a "sorry" shrug, but by the time my hands stopped shaking on the steering wheel he was long gone. Swallowed by the darkness.

Once again I was alone on a road that looked so good when I first over-wrote the GPS parameters on my iPhone and changed "fastest route" and "highways" to "least traffic".

Well, that part was sure right. There wasn't another vehicle in sight.

No headlights and no street lights, just darkness, alleviated only by the small sliver of a crescent moon and millions of hard, bright stars glittering like shards of broken glass scattered across a black velvet tapestry.

I took a breath of the cooling night air rushing past, whipping around me in the slipstream. I considered putting the top up on my meticulously restored '69 Firebird 400 but the air was still warm from the desert heat of the day, though I knew that as soon as that dissipated, the temperature would fall quickly.

That doesn't matter. Stifling another yawn I shook my head. *Long before that, I've gotta get off the road and get some sleep or I'm gonna end my return from Vegas in a ditch rather than the Hollywood Hills.*

Yeah, I needed to find a motel or something and get some rest. Maybe a Marriott or Ramada or Holiday Inn or even a Motel 6... anything. But where?

I recalled remarking to a girlfriend as we munched popcorn on the couch in front of the latest TV horror flick, "What kind of an idiot pulls over to sleep on a road in the middle of nowhere?"

Apparently one exactly like me, because If I didn't find somewhere in the next few miles, that was exactly what I was going to have to do.

I could picture the perky blond reporter for the local news standing in front of my convertible, top slashed and mottled in my blood. "Police were horrified this morning to find the bloody remains of the former well-known rock star, apparently butchered sometime late last night by the serial killer some are calling the, "Desert Highway Slasher."

Just great. I wasn't sure what bothered me most about my grim fantasy - the imagined grisly death or snarky epitaph of "former well-known rock star".

I'm still doing well-paid gigs on the 'oldies' circuit, aren't I? My career isn't over yet, is it? I'm not a 'former star' - or am I?

I sighed at that last thought.

I really had nothing to complain about. After all, hadn't I been lead singer and rhythm guitar for one of the biggest bands to come out of the '60s and '70s? In fact, we kept recording and turning out hits all through the 80 and 90's, appearing with the biggest names in stadium rock and well into the 2000's when the nostalgia tours ramped up.

People still came up after every show saying, "Dude, we remember going to your concert in St. Louis (or Boston, or Tampa, or Philly) on our first date." Except now those former teenage sweethearts had double chins, saggy skin, and white hair.

Another sigh.

I shook my head again. My mind kept drifting. I had to find someplace soon.

***

I began slowing to check the hard-packed dirt on the right hand roadside for turnouts when I noticed a faint reddish blush in the distance on the far left-hand side of the road.

Is it a town or gas station or some sort of human habitation? And if so, can I even make it that far?

I flashed back on my vision of my own lonely demise and got a new burst of determination. Something sounded better than a long cold night in the car haunted by visions of slashers.

I pushed down on the pedal again.

***

It was only another 20 minutes or so but it felt like hours. Driving and driving I never seemed to get any closer. But eventually - finally - I began to make out the shape of a sprawling building rising up through the reddish glow of a thousand twinkling lights reflecting from the night sky.

As I drew closer I was amazed at the size of the building stuck out here in the back of beyond with nothing around for at least 100 miles in any direction.

Downshifting I turned off the blacktop and down a long brick driveway toward a two-story stucco topped by a graceful, sweeping arched portico of the old Spanish Mission style - right down to the antique bell framed in the soft glow of a red spotlight above the porte-cochere.

What is this place?

It looked like a hotel or large motel but I couldn't see any of the well-known corporate chain logos anywhere. No matter. The closer I got the more convinced I became that it was some kind of a hotel and at this point, I'd take a moldy old army cot.

I pulled into the nearly deserted parking lot to the right of the main entrance and as I stepped around the other side of the car to grab my overnight bag I noticed the sign, small and discrete, just to the left of the double doors.

It was made of some kind of dark stone with faded gold letters that read; "Welcome to the Hotel Cal……."

There were two small lights, one on either side, to illuminate the lettering. The light on the right half of the sign had apparently burned out and that side remained obscure against the dark stone.

I shrugged. I didn't care what the name was as long as they had a bed and a hot shower and maybe if I was lucky a bottle of something cold.

I pulled open the brass handled door and went inside

***

The first thing I noticed was that despite the late hour there was a uniformed desk clerk waiting attentively behind the long, polished dark oak counter.

His gaze never left me as I let the door swing shut behind me and made my way across the colorful Spanish-tiled lobby until I stood before him.

"I'd like a room if you've got…"

"Yes, sir," he answered smoothly before I even had a chance to complete the sentence. "We've been expecting you."

"Expecting me?"

I was baffled.

"I didn't even know I was stopping here until ten minutes ago."

"Nevertheless," he continued, the smile never leaving his face , "we were told you'd be checking in tonight."

"By whom?"

What kind of bullshit is this?

He looked down at a blue-lined index card he was holding and replied, "It doesn't say, sir. I just found a reservation request on the desk when I came in tonight. But if you would be so kind, please check it over to make sure that all of the particulars are correct and if so, then merely sign it and I can give you your key."

He held up an ornate brass key on a red velvet ribbon. The number 217 was etched into the handle.

Who made the reservation? Was it through a web site or direct? A phone call or email? They must have some sort of a record. He has to be lying.

I studied the clerk's face more carefully. The smile was sincere, though a little bland. A black suit with thin red piping around the lapels. His hair was black with a smattering of grey, medium length and parted in the middle. He was leaning forward on his elbows but looked to be of medium height too, 5' 9" or 5' 10".

He could have been anywhere between 40 to 60 and appeared not at all concerned about my scrutiny. He was patience personified.

I looked at the blue index card with all of my particulars laid out neatly and correct. Name, address - even my cell phone. *How did they get that? I never give it out.*

"Would you like the bellman to help you with your luggage sir?" He inquired with that same solicitous, measured tone.

I glanced down at my glorified gym bag which contained nothing more than a shirt, a few T-shirts, underwear and shaving gear.

"No - all I got is this," I said, holding up the bag.

He nodded and suddenly I was very tired.

I yawned and stretched my shoulders. Then flipped the blue card around and scrawled my signature on the bottom.

He whisked the card off the counter with his left hand and with the right held out the old-fashioned brass key.

"It's number 217. At the top of the stairs and two doors down on the right hand side."

I took the key and stooped to pick up my bag.

"Oh - sir?"

I straightened up and looked back at him. He was holding a cream-colored envelope in his right hand.

"I almost forgot. This was also left for you."

"By who?" I asked suspiciously.

Again the shrug and apologetic smile. "Sorry, sir. It was here when I came on duty tonight."

I took the proffered envelope. It was thick and heavy with my name written on the front in elaborate Elizabethan style calligraphy.

I was about to rip it open but instead stuffed it into my back pocket, nodded goodnight to the clerk and headed for the stairs.

As I crossed the lobby I noticed again how everything seemed to be in what the old movies would have called the 'Spanish Mission' style of pastel yellow adobe walls ornamented with grey weathered-wood framed paintings of southwest desert scenes which contrasted nicely with lighted alcoves filled with Native American artwork and turquoise figurines. I passed under a massive wrought-iron chandelier with dozens of tapered candelabra bulbs glowing softly and had just put my foot on the first step when I thought I heard a voice from behind me say, "Have fun."

I turned around but there was no one there. The desk was deserted and the only person in the lobby was me.

I continued up the stairs.

***

It wasn't a room... it was a friggin' suite.

Big bay windows overlooked the pool and beyond that the dark starlit desert stretched away to the inky black smudge of low foothills. I stood there for a minute scanning the horizon for a little light that would indicate any other human habitation for the next twenty miles. Nothing. The darkness stretched off to impenetrable infinity. *Kinda' like my life.*

I sighed and pulled the curtain closed. I glanced around the room.

Spanish lace hung from a four-poster king-size bed. The dark gilded wood furniture featured Spanish influence as well. A full bar with a fridge and breakfast nook stood across from a large TV housed in an elaborate cabinet of the same dark wood and black leather couch. As I passed by the TV I noticed that for all the opulence of the room the set itself was one of the massive CRT tube kinds that had gone out of style twenty years ago. *How strange – haven't they heard of flat panel?*

The spacious bathroom boasted a black onyx look bathtub that sported a dozen jacuzzi jets. Though nice, it couldn't compare to some of the outrageous hotel rooms I'd visited in New York, London, Paris, Tokyo or Dubai back when our band was touring, but it was pretty damn good for somewhere smack dab in the middle of nowhere - even if it was about twenty years out of date.

Yeah, all in all not bad for a desert motel - or hotel - or... whatever?

I yawned again and padded over to the bar.

To my surprise, the fridge held not only beer and wine but some Jack, Irish and even champagne as well.

I pulled out the cold bottle of fizz and was just about to pop the cork when I noticed it was pink - then I noticed the label and something inside me recoiled way deep down.

I couldn't have rightly said what it was but I suspected that there was some residual drunken, debauched fuck-up - both literally and figuratively - that stirred an atavistic memory from some pre-show, post-show, no-show, party lurking somewhere in my deep, dark jumble of confused rock n' roll memory. And odds were if it was like most of them, it was nothing worthy of dredging up.

I put the bottle back and popped a Heineken instead. I slouched down on the couch and turning on the TV, tilted my head back for a long welcome swig, draining half the bottle.

I thought briefly of unpacking until I realized that I had nothing to unpack.

When everything was rolled into a ball and stuffed into a duffle bag, what was the point of unpacking?

Like I was gonna' change into anything - after all, I wasn't going anywhere.

I closed my eyes.

Of course, I was wrong.

***

I opened my eyes and looked at the digital clock under the TV. It was blinking and the TV was off.

Must have lost power for a minute.

Well, this was officially the middle of nowhere.

Might as well move to the bed and get a proper rest.

I stood up, stripped off my T-shirt and unbuckled my jeans. That's when I felt it - the envelope in my back pocket.

I pulled it out and looked at it again.

The same fancy calligraphy embossed with my name. I ripped it open.

"Ms. Jennifer DeMarney Howard requests the pleasure of your company this evening at her 'Soirée D'artiste'.

Please join us at your convenience in the 'Mirror Salon'.

The Soirée runs from dusk til' dawn and we can guarantee you the finest wines, most tempting tidbits, stimulating conversation, tempting companionship and all of your favorite music. It is an evening you cannot afford to miss."

It was signed with an elaborate flowing signature; "Jennifer DeMarney Howard."

WTF…?

What the hell is this?

Who was this woman and what did she want with me? I didn't even know her and she was inviting me to some strange party in a hotel I'd never heard, of in a place I'd never been to, at the ass-end of nowhere, in the middle of the fuckin' night!

I was about to toss the invitation into the ornate wastebasket when there was a sharp rap on the door.

What now?

I sighed, buckled my jeans and slightly pissed yanked open the door.

There was no one there.

I looked down the hall. No one.

I started to close the door when I saw a pink post-it note.

It was written in the same elaborate calligraphy and read, "Are you coming?"

***

I had actually decided I was not.

And unlike most of the bad decisions which have congealed into an amorphous mass of vague regrets over a lifetime, this one on the face of it appeared as though it was made for all the right reasons.

It was late, although just how late I was not exactly sure. Like I said, sometime while I'd dozed off the power had gone out and now all the clocks, damn their digital souls, were merely flashing their red, green and white LED digits in a meaningless mishmash of indecipherable and irrelevant numbers. Likewise, the 10-year battery on my 2-year-old watch had evidently decided that this would be an appropriate time to give up the ghost to complete my total sense of disorientation from the constructs of the real world.

In other words, I had no idea what fuckin' time it was.

Reason number 2: I was tired. No question there.

Large and loud growling yawns combined with all too recent memories of falling asleep at the wheel.

Yup - I was way overdue for a "long winters nap."

Reason three. I had to be back in LA by noon tomorrow for rehearsal for our new album.

Here I paused. I wasn't speaking to Rolling Stone or a late Nite TV Show. There was no one to impress or lie to but me. And I already knew the truth - way too well.

No one - and I mean no one, was really gonna be interested in a new album of songs by a bunch of old Rock n' Rollers whose best work had been done a full generation ago.

Let's face it, the new stuff was a 'throw-away' by our label to keep us happy.

"Make the ol' dudes think they're still relevant and that the industry actually gives a shit about anything new they might come up with."

They knew as well as we did that our real value to them was in the nostalgia tours where we made aging flower children forget their arthritis and sagging bellies for a night.

I walked over to the gilt-framed mirror and stared at the image in the low wattage light. That was the way I preferred to use the mirror now. Low wattage.

That way I didn't have to see all the lines in the face. Circles around the eyes. Sags under the chin. Jowls in what used to be described as a 'firm jaw' and what was now referred to as a 'rugged macho look' by the unshaven young studs, on me seemed more reminiscent of the grey stubbled look of the Bowery bums of my childhood.

Charming.

Yeah - every mature thought of my far too mature brain screamed, "hey you sad old bastard, hang it up. Go to bed and crash for whatever is left of the night. Get up and get an early start tomorrow and make it to the studio on time. Who cares if the new stuff is any good? It doesn't matter - you can tour forever on your classic singles and helping other old former hippies recall those halcyon days when they ruled the world and vowed to, "never trust anyone over 30."

I laughed to myself - or was it at myself?

Either way, it was good advice. Go to bed.

I wish that I had taken it.

***

In the end that same old curiosity that caused Pandora to open the box and has been killing off kitty cats from time immemorial had its way with me and I went.

I'm not sure what I'd expected but it was nothing like it and maybe everything.

***

First, there was the room.

A typical hotel function room and yet I had to admit that they (whoever 'they' were) had done a great job with the decorations. Something like a cross between a "Hard Rock Cafe" and Haight Ashbury crash pad - that is if the crash pad had been held in a faded Nob Hill mansion.

The walls were festooned with old R-n'-R posters from the California 'glory days'. Joplin, Hendricks, Jeff Airplane, The Doors,

Fleetwood Mac, as well as signed publicity photos and memorabilia ... drums, keyboards, mics, tambourines and an impressive collection of all kinds of classic guitars. Everting from Fender Strats to Martin acoustic Dreadnoughts.

I took all that in during the first 30 seconds after I walked through the open door of what the ubiquitous desk clerk had labeled, "The Gold Room".

The second thing I noticed were the mirrors.

It was hard not to.

They covered the entire ceiling.

In fact, it was somewhat disorienting every time I looked up to see not just the motion of moving bodies but a constantly swirling ripple of motion - sort of like ghosts drifting in and out of reality.

***

I don't know how long I stood there or why I expected that there would be someone to greet me at the door, or know who I was, or even give a shit about it.

I should have developed a more realistic expectation of the realities of life by now I reflected as I finally moved from the doorway into the noise and unsettling swirl of color that seemed to revolve around the preternaturally large interior of what should have been a standard hotel function room.

I tried to make my way unobtrusively through the various groups of conversations throughout the satellites of strangely static knots of people who seemed oddly poised - as though waiting for some cosmic director to instruct them as to where to stand and what to say.

I wanted nothing more than to be unobtrusive. To move through the faceless crowd and babbling voices to...what?

As I wandered aimlessly, deeper into the room a few apparently began to recognize me.

First one raised eyebrow, then a whisper. Then one smiled at me. Then another. Soon everyone was nodding. A few gave me fist pumps, passionless hugs, and perfunctory compliments. But it was bullshit. All of it.

They were not really happy I was here.

These were not old-time fans.

Half were the typical Hollywood 'pretty boys' and 'party girls', and the other half looked like a cartoonish collection of balding producers, slick agents and silicone-enhanced models that had graced every sybaritic party since I first came west from Dayton, Ohio in 1969.

Then I'd been a typical college dropout. Just another garage band kid from the mid-west with more balls than talent. Too dumb to understand that just because you could sing, play a few chords and write some songs that people liked to sing along with you could make it in the music biz.

But that's how it had worked out.

Maybe not the very top but a couple of hit albums, a good long run and then the re-runs with the nostalgia tour.

Those were the good parts.

I tried not to dwell on the not so good.

Unfortunately, the latter seemed to be replacing the former more frequently now.

Was it second thoughts, regret for things done or left undone or maybe just the inevitable and inescapable decay of an aging rock and roller - or perhaps all of the above?

Shit.

"Is it really that bad?"

I stopped.

Had what I'd thought were only thoughts been said out loud?

Maybe.

I obviously hadn't been paying much attention.

I'd circled through the room, passing in and out of chattering bunches of inconsequential conversations like a ghost until, quite unknown to me, I'd wound up in front of a small ornate table, flanked by a red and gold flock upholstered Queen Ann chair situated like a throne at the back of the room.

I turned and looked over my shoulder to where the voice had come from and saw her.

A girl.

And not just any girl.

A girl who looked like she'd been cobbled together from all my dreams. A living embodiment of all the girls I'd ever have and all the ones I hadn't but wished I had.

She was blond with long hair that curled around her shoulders, a heart-shaped oval face-framing wide green eyes that seemed innocent and erotic all at the same time. Her body was slight and willowy but with a hint of voluptuousness that teased from amidst the long black dress of leather and lace that swirled around her like the wings of a dark angel.

And obviously, I wasn't the only one who noticed. The entire room seemed to revolve around her - like the omnipresent rotation of planets around the sun, by the coalescing of those sycophantic bodies around a single human celestial star.

She looked at me with disingenuous amusement for a long moment before holding out a black lace covered hand as if to be kissed.

I did.

"My name is Rhiannon," she said.

Of course.

***

Everyone has a 'dream love' who embodies all of the hoped-for but never achieved fantasies of love, romance lust, and infatuation that we half-believe and hope for but realize right from the get-go that we will never have.

Since the first caveman drew a pic of some fantasy babe with giant boobs and booty, all of human-kind has always fantasied about love.

Girls had their 'knights in shining armor'. Cinderella had her prince.

Poor boys had the 'Princess', the beautiful heiress, and both sexes had movie stars, models and of course, 'Rock Stars'.

For me, as a kid from Ohio trying to crack the tinsel ceiling of the LA rock scene of the early 70's it had been the girl I'd met at a post-album launch party in the mid-70's - Stevie Nicks.

She was cute, funny and had the sexiest most evocative voice I'd ever heard.

She was also deeply involved with someone else. So we chatted for ten minutes, promised to 'get together sometime', and never did.

But forever after she was my template for 'the Girl', that I was looking for.

And strange as it sounds, I found her.

Over and over and over...

Yeah - that's what we do.

Maybe famous philosophers say it best - mine was Jackson Brown with his line... "we'll fill in the missing colors in each other's paint-by-number dreams."

Yup.

So you know what's coming next.

Right. I spent the rest of my life looking for my, 'Stevie'.

Beautiful, blond, romantic, sexy and witchy woman style in equal portions but most of all... that voice. That incredible smoky, sexy voice.

And to quote another prince of MTV, forever asking, "Where can I find a woman like that?"

And then, quite out of nowhere, I did.

It happened on a southern swing.

Whenever we toured we still needed backup singers to replace the studio girls who sang chorus and overdubbed on our albums and later CD's.

But when we went off on the road the label managers and sharp-pencil guys wanted us to scarf up local talent who would work for pennies on the dollar just to tour a few hick cities with a West Coast name band.

That's where I met Juniper.

She'd left college in her junior year to and was hanging out in Nashville trying to land a singing gig in one of the many bars.

When I met her she was trying to make rent money by filling in as a backup singer for recording studios and touring bands - like us.

I first noticed her for her looks. She had long blond hair, big green eyes and pouty pink lips that begged to be kissed.

But what really attracted me most was not her looks, although to describe her as adorable was an understatement.

No, it was her voice that knocked me out the first time she hit those high harmonies on the chorus of our opening number.

She was quite honestly the best 'back-up babe' I'd ever heard in ours or any bands. And by the time we'd finished our opening gig in Nashville, I was 'madly' in love with her. Note the quotes around the words, "Madly".

We'd become an item and she became my lady and for almost a year, toured with us, even moving in with me when we came back to LA and started working on our next album.

That's probably what caused things to fall apart.

When you're writing songs and testing them out there's really not a whole lot for backup singers to do.

Of course, by this time she wanted to be more than a backup singer and I naturally wanted that for her too.

At least that's what I said.

And I think I meant it too.

I even wrote a song for her and tried it with the band and it was good - really good.

because she was really good too. Maybe not 'rock n' roll diva' good - not yet, but a damn sight better than most of the talent of the day.

She was thrilled with the idea of becoming a part of the band with what might be the title track on the new album.

But when it came time to choose the final tracks our manager, Vincent, called us in - just us.

He lit one of those rank Mexican cigarillo's he always smoked and said, "Hey guys, you need to make a choice here. She's good you know. Maybe too good."

"What do you mean?" I didn't like the way this was going.

"I mean that you guys wouldn't be the first band to find that the cute little eye candy with the 1,000 watt smile and dynamite voice that they thought was just the female vocalist had become what the audience came to see, and a little while later woke up to find themselves known only as "Her Band"."

And that was how it all fell apart.

I knew that I should have taken a stand. I should have told them, "Hey - fuck you! We're a set. You take her or you don't get me."

Yeah, that's what I should have told them.

But I didn't - I'd worked too hard. We all had.

And deep down we knew that what Vincent, as full of shit as he usually was, was right. She was cute enough and good enough to go star quality in her own right. And where would that leave us? Junipers Band.

Oh, I could have tried to start a new band or formed a duo with her but as in love as I was with her I still had enough sense to remember that singing duo's and lovers more often than not, never seem to last.

We didn't either.

We tried. We really did. I even wrote her some more songs and got her gigs at clubs and sang with her until Vincent's two-minute call reminded me that appearing with another act without the labels permission was a breach of contract and I could either desist or hit the bricks. I desisted.

First, she was hurt - then she got mad - then we split.

We did try to get back together. Lots of tears, promises to never fight again and great make-up sex, but it didn't last. It never does.

After a while we drifted apart. She moved to SF and cut an album with a small independent label. She sent me a copy.

It was good because she was good. But she was still trying to make it as a single and her folky style was on its way out in the seventies and as time passed we lost touch and I never heard what became of her.

All this ran through my head in an instant because the cute little thing in front of me looked almost the way she had the last time I'd seen her.

It was uncanny - change the clothes and the hairstyle and...

***

"Humm..." She cocked her head and laid one small, white finger on her cheek. "Either my beauty has left you speechless or I've grown a second head."

"Definitely the former," I smiled, a touch embarrassed and more than a little intrigued. "Rhiannon. Nice name and a great song. Was your mom a Fleetwood Mac fan?"

"Absolutely, especially Buckingham and Nicks. She even bought their first solo album because she thought their cover was 'daring' for expressing 'naked love'."

"Well, it certainly was that," I smiled remembering the nude pose cover that few saw and even fewer bought before they went on to join Fleetwood Mac and make musical history.

"And so you became Rhiannon who, "rings like a bell through the night'."

"And, 'Wouldn't you love to love her?'" She grinned back.

"Absolutely." I could smell her perfume. It smelled like incense and peppermints. "Can I start by buying you a drink?"

***

There was a champagne fountain in the middle of the room but I hated pink champagne so we made our way to a small bar in the corner where I got a Jack and she a glass of Pinot Grigio.

"So what is this party all about?" I asked looking around at the somewhat frenetic crowd who seemed to be more interesting in projecting the image of having fun than actually having it.

She raised her eyebrows. "Oh, I thought you knew. It's for my mother's birthday. Didn't you see it on the invitation?"

"No. I got an invitation but it didn't say anything about a birthday party, just an invitation to be here."

"Well, I'm glad you're here and hope you'll be staying for the feast."

Feast...?

I wanted to ask her about her rather strange choice of words but she took my hand and with a dazzling hundred-watt smile led me to one desperately frenetic group of partygoers after another.

And after a while, the strange term of "feast" started seeming not so strange after all because the look under the facile smiles and mindless chatter could only be described as... hungry.

But for what I didn't know.

Finally, despite Rhiannon's innocent/erotic charm, I felt that if I didn't get out of the cloying cloud of sycophancy I was going to explode.

"Look," I said turning to her, "does this hotel have a bar or any place we can get away from this crowd for a little while?"

She cocked her head to one side, opened her adorable eyes wide and asked with breathless mock concern, "Why - you mean you're not having the time of your life being dragged from one scintillating group of BP's to another?"

"BP's?"

She tugged my collar and bought my right ear close to her pink lips whispering, "Beautiful People."

"Ah... yeah."

She stepped back and took both of my hand in hers and cocked her head to one side.

She considered me for a moment and then broke into a little tinkling laugh that reminded me of something lost long ago.

"Oh don't look so sad!"

She turned on her heal but kept hold of my right hand and winked over her shoulder. "Come on - I know just the place."

***

I followed behind her in a kind of daze, watching her slim form glide back through the lobby, then up the stairs, down the corridor until she stopped in front of a door.

The door to a room.

My room.

***

I was both surprised and not at all when she closed the door by pushing me up against it and pressed herself into my arms.

Not surprised because this was far from my first rodeo and I knew the moves from a thousand groupies who had trooped through a thousand hotel rooms in search of bragging rights about being, "with the band".

And surprised because this seemed like a girl who had no need to.

Add that to the fact that while no teeny-bopper she still was obviously young enough to be my …

She raised her head and peered up at me. "Hmmm… the expected response at this point is usually to kiss me."

"Are you sure that you want to…?"

She put one soft finger to my lips and whispered, "A wise man it is said asks no questions but accepts the gifts laid before him with a happy heart."

"Who said that - Confucius?"

"No - me."

I'd like to say that for once in my life I did the right thing. Told her she was too young for me and whatever daddy issues she was having by bedding an older guy could be better working out on an analysts couch than between my sheets. But I didn't.

I never do.

I'd also like to say that I felt extremely guilty afterward but I didn't.

I felt great, in fact, I felt better than I had in years - almost as though I'd slipped into some time warp and was once again a contemporary of delightfully sparkling, free spirits with the soft creamy skin of the adorable young woman beside me.

Still… I had to ask it. The question that had been nagging me ever since she stopped in front of the door to my room.

"Why?"

She propped her head up on her hand and leaned into the pillow.

"Why?"

"Yeah - why me?"

She smiled and her eyes crinkled. "Why not you?"

"Well, I can't help thinking that a girl like you could have her choice of whole lot younger, cooler and more interesting guys than this ol' fart rock n' roller."

Her face grew serious and she pursed her lips as she seemed to consider this for a long moment.

Then the smile returned as she drew my face close to hers and whispered, "Perhaps - but they're not you. You're special."

And she kissed me.

***

It might have been my nagging sense of guilt competing with my equally strong sense of satisfaction and incredible luck but when we returned to the party it seemed as though the entire room was exchanging glances that fairly smirked, "Yeah, we know what you've been up to."

For a moment I almost considered leaving a getting some much-needed rest but in the same instant, she squeezed my hand and whispered, "Don't pay any attention. They live for salacious gossip."

A wicked little grin played across her lips. "So let's give them some."

And with that leaned into me a gave me a long and lascivious kiss.

When we broke and I glanced up I was surprised that far from being surprised or outraged the look that flashed from face to face around the room seemed to be... pleased.

Especially the older woman sitting at the back of the room.

The smile that played around her too red lips was one of intense satisfaction.

As we drifted through the milling crowd, their faces were expectant but their eyes were gleaming bright and almost… feral.

They parted silently but then seemed to close back around us like white blood cells surrounding a virus they are preparing to ingest.

The skin on the back of my neck began to prickle.

We continued on with what seemed to be interminable slowness for an infinite amount of time down the length of an impossible long mahogany table set with gleaming silver forks and intricately filigreed knives.

Finally, after what could have been an instant or eternity, the end of the table was not so much as reached as appeared before us.

Rhiannon squeezed my hand and inclined her head to the seated figure at the tables head.

"Mother this is…" She let the introduction trail off and squeezed my hand tighter as she glanced down at the seated figure. Without looking back at me she continued in her low throaty voice. "And of course, this is my mother."

***

I stared at the slender figure seated in the massive chair that looked like it had been carved from the same wood as the long table.

She was dressed in a long flowing dress of black silk festooned about the waist, shoulders, and sleeves with dark red velvet ribbons.

Her hair was covered by an elaborate lace mantilla and fine mesh veil, also a deep onyx black, which blurred her features.

She sat immobile for what could have been a second or an hour. Then she raised her right hand, half covered by the flowing lace of her dress and dominated by a large blood-red ruby on her ring finger.

The hand bent forward at the wrist and once again, the only thing I could think of to do was what I'd seen in dozens of movies where I saw that same gesture.

I kissed it.

The small hand lingered in mine for a moment and then pulled back.

It paused by the side of her face and then slowly drew back the veil and let it drape around her shoulders.

She was beautiful.

Not as beautiful as her daughter Rhiannon, but I could instantly see that Rhiannon had got most of her looks from her mother and probably very little from whoever her father had been.

Her mother had the same coloring, soft white skin, and eyes.

Oh, certainly there were some wrinkles, sags and crow's feet but they had been artfully minimized by very effective make-up. Especially the eyes - which were large, dark, and luminous.

Those eyes held mine for what seemed like hours until her lips finally formed a crooked smile.

"Welcome." She said, in a voice, an octave lower but still reminiscent of her daughter's. "Welcome to my birthday party - you're just in time for the feast."

There was that word again... feast. Who nowadays calls any kind of meal a ... feast?

I was aware of a soft shuffling of feet behind me and turned to see that the ubiquitous crowd had moved behind us and were now leaning forward on the dozens of chars surrounding the table, gripping the backs with expressions of hungry expectation.

As if she could read my thoughts Rhiannon's mother smiled and nodded to me.

"Yes," She breathed out in that same melodious but husky voice, 'the feast.' They are so very hungry and they've been waiting so very long."

She held my gaze a moment longer before glancing at her daughter and inclining her head.

"Rhiannon dear, and I do believe it's time. Will you please complete the arrangements and bring out the feast?

Rhiannon smiled. "Finally," she sighed.

I couldn't help it. Without even thinking I blurted out, "Just what the hell is this, 'feast?'"

Her mother turned back to me.

"Soon," she whispered. "Soon everything will be clear. Just as it was always meant to be."

"What the hell is she talking about?" I turned to Rhiannon but all I caught was a glimpse of her retreating back before she slid behind a dark curtain at the rear of the room.

"Where's she going?" I was getting pissed - and a little - no make that a lot! ... creeped out.

"Why to prepare the feast of course." The corners of her mouth turned up and her dark eyes sparkled from beneath dark purple lids.

I opened my mouth to ask the same question again but realized I'd just get another circular answer.

The room lights flickered.

Then I noticed they were off and the only illumination was from a dozen sets of blood-red candles lined in a vertical row down the center of the long dark table.

What the fuck was I doing here?

Why was I still here?

The entire scene had passed beyond strange into Twilight Zone weirdness, and guess what...? I didn't need this shit.

It was time to do what I'd always done best. Leave.

I turned back to the "witchy" Queen.

"Look - sorry, but I've been up for twelve hours and I'm due for a major crash. So if you don't mind, make my apologies to Rhiannon and tell her maybe we'll connect back in LA sometime."

"You haven't changed at all, have you?"

"What? Changed? How do you mean?"

"You're still the same old Rock N" Roll egotist you were forty years ago."

She was staring at me with a look that I had known before - from a long time before.

I stared back. And the longer I did the more my memories began to swirl - forming, re-forming and finally congealing around a nagging core of recognition.

I knew her.

Beneath the black silk, lace, and makeup there was a girl I recognized.

"You - you're …"

"Jennifer," she said, her eyes never leaving me.

I shook my head.

"No, not Jennifer…"

"Juniper." She supplied.

"Yessss…" the word hissed off my tongue.

Of course, I knew it.

It was me who'd coined that name for her.

She had told me the night we'd met, over bad wine, good weed, and better sex, that the name she'd been born with was Jennifer but she'd always wanted something better. Something unique. Something dramatic. Something poetic. Something that she'd want to use on stage with someone like me.

So that night I'd changed Jennifer to Juniper in honor of another of the 60's poet/songwriters, to Donavan's, "Jennifer, Juniper".

That was the night she became Juniper and my girlfriend.

Until it all fell apart.

***

It came back all in a rush.

The love. The pain.

The jealousy.

The break-up.

And...

"Juniper - I mean Jennifer." My throat felt dry - constricted. "Where have you been? What have you been doing? I mean what have you been up to for ..."

"The last forty years?" she finished, her expression unreadable.

All I could do was nod.

"Do you remember the night you left me?"

I did but I didn't want to.

She knew it.

"Do you remember what I told you after I caught you in our bedroom with that sixteen-year-old groupie?"

I tried to shake my head but we both knew it was a lie.

One of many I'd told her.

"I told you that you couldn't leave. I told you that it was time for you to finally grow up.

I told you that you didn't have to create the band we'd always dreamed of but you did need to take responsibility for the first time in your life. I told you that I loved you."

Her voice turned soft and her eyes glistened for a moment before they turned into hard obsidian chips and her voice turned just as cold and brittle. "I told you all of that, and just before you panicked and walked out for good, I told you that I was pregnant."

***

I thought of a thousand things to say, each lamer and more self-serving than the last, so in the end I said nothing. Not even sorry. Because that was the lamest of all.

She continued - her voice drifting from cold to warm and nostalgic to bitter as she recounted the almost two years we spent as lovers, dreamers, musical partners and finally a pair of rivals caught somewhere between love and regret.

But she was right. In the end, I did leave her.

And I did cheat on her.

And I did take the band into which we had just begun morphing our romantic duet.

After all, how can you sing romantic songs when the romance has gone. The audience can always spot a fraud.

But I shouldn't have done it that way.

I couldn't be a hypocrite and say I shouldn't have cheated.

I was in LA in the 70's - the time of "Boogey Nights", and everybody was.

But I shouldn't have done it like that. In our bed, with a groupie.

It was like I almost wanted to get caught and I probably did - just to add a punctuation mark at the end of our sentence. Finis.

But I didn't know she was pregnant.

"No." I finally said. "You never told me you were pregnant."

She cocked her head and stared up at me for a long moment.

Finally, she gave me a half-smile and said, "You know, I almost think that you believe that."

I started to open my mouth but she waved her hand. "No matter. All that is past. Long past." She settled back into the throne-like oak chair and stared at me from beneath dark lashes. "Now all that is left is for us to celebrate the results of those long past days with our entire reason for gathering here tonight."

She reached down beside her and her hand came up holding a tambourine. It was made of dark wood with silver cymbals and multicolored ribbons hanging from the rim.

I recognized it.

It was her tambourine from when we had performed together.

She shook it with a flourish and slapped the heal of her right and against worn brown skin of the head.

"Bing in the feast," she cried.

And the faceless crowd ringing the table echoed, "The feast."

The curtains parted behind her and Rhiannon returned bearing a large silver platter with an ornate silver cover. She set it before her mother and then stepped back to retrieve a carved box from a man standing behind her.

Her mother stood up and Rhiannon placed the box in front her, moving over to one side and placing her had on the lid of the platter.

Her mother, my former Jennifer/Juniper, nodded to her daughter and they both fixed their eyes on me.

Then Rhiannon removed the lid.

One voice in the room said, "What the fuck?"

One set of feet took two stumbling steps backward.

They were mine.

On the platter surrounded by garnishes of fruits and raw vegetables was a baby. A new-born baby.

It didn't cry. It didn't make a sound. It just fixed its eyes on mine.

I tried to speak but nothing came out.

Finally, I shook my head and said again, "What the fuck? What is it all of this?"

No one spoke.

Rhiannon bent and undid the catches of the ornate wooden box and opened it for her mother.

It contained a long gleaming knife, fork and sharpening steel nestled in deep red velvet. A carving set.

Jennifer pick up the knife and gave it several quick swipes against the sharpening steel, then put down the steel and picked up the wickedly pointed two tined carving fork.

She leaned forward until the instruments hovered over the staring infant.

I froze in horror.

Jennifer paused and looked at me.

"Oh - where are my manners. Isn't the job of the father to carve the meat?"

She held out the knife and fork to me.

"Well isn't it - Papa?"

"Papa! What the fuck are you talking about?"

I took a step backward.

"She smiled at me.

Her teeth gleamed white against her pale face.

White and small and pointed.

"Why yes, my love. Haven't you guessed? This is your child."

"Mine? But you told me you were pregnant when I left you. That was years ago!"

"Yes." She nodded. "And tonight, you met the offspring of that pregnancy - your daughter." She looked at the young woman standing beside her. "Your daughter - and tonight your lover - Rhiannon."

I realized that I was shaking my head in disbelief, but I couldn't stop. *My daughter…*

Finally, I managed to whisper. "But this baby - where did it come from? Whose is it? You're not going to try to tell me that somehow it's…"

"Yes - it is. Yours."

"The cosmic offspring of you and the daughter you never knew all manifested here. In this place where time and reality have no place."

"What do you mean?" I couldn't think. My brain was seeking a dark hole to scamper into.

"Do you remember about twenty years ago there was a Hollywood wrap party held at a remote desert inn for the cast and crew of an unimportant little "B" flick?" She shook her head. "Most people don't. It wasn't a very good movie but both I and your daughter had small parts in it."

She paused and her features along with the those in the room seemed to waver like an out of focus picture before they coalesced and sharpened again.

She continued, "Later that night, after the banquet, when most of the cast had fallen asleep or passed out, a fire broke out. The fire marshal said perhaps it was faulty wiring or from one of the candles on the banquet table, but it spread quickly and many of the cast died before help could arrive.

"We are that cast."

There was a sigh, like an intake of breath or a damp wind.

"So every year we gather to celebrate that feast. But this year we received a very special guest to help us celebrate."

"A guest of honor. You. So what could be more fitting that we all consume the fruits of your actions - the manifestation of your selfish, self-centered life. It's time for your sacrifice to nourish the spirits of all those casually used in life."

She handed me the knife and fork. "Carve."

***

I ran.

I don't remember starting. I don't remember even finding the door.

I just remember the gleaming eyes. The wet lips and hungry smiles.

So I ran... down the impossibly long hallway, lengthening my stride past room after room now filled with laughing, chattering, partying people who all looked the same... vacant, shallow and empty.

Finally after what seemed to be hours I saw a sign over a set of double doors that read, "Lobby."

Gratefully I pushed through the doors and almost ran up to the front desk. Without a pause I slammed my hand down on the old fashioned desk bell, barked out to the deserted lobby "Hey - whoever you are - wherever you are - that's it!. I'm outta' here!"

For a desperate moment, I imagined the desk clerk was gone. And the front door would be bolted. I'd be an eternal prisoner of the never-ending party. Doomed to search in vain through rooms filled with smiling faces and lifeless, soulless eyes.

I considered running for the door and glanced over my shoulder - would it be locked?

When I turned back the clerk was standing there behind the desk - smiling his inscrutable smile as though he'd always been there and always would be.

"Yes sir, and how may I help you this morning?"

Morning?

I glanced toward the plate glass window across the lobby and sure enough, the pitch-black was beginning to lighten to a fuzzy grey/blue tinged with hints of gold.

"I'm leaving. Checking out. Getting the hell outta' here"

"But sir," He smiled with his infuriatingly bland smile, "your suite and all charges have been taken care of and its' not even check out time. Please," he held out his hand and gestured back toward the long corridor. "The party continues and they're all waiting for you." He raised one eyebrow as he accentuated the word, "you."

I shifted my bag on my shoulder and opened my mouth to tell him what I thought of him, the hotel and the whole of perverse humanity but in the end, all I could mutter was, "Fuck them - and fuck you too."

I crossed the lobby and called back over my shoulder, "Do what you want about the room. Give it to the next asshole who wanders into this Twilight Zone by mistake but I'm checking out and you can't stop me."

He called after me, "Oh, please don't give it a second thought, sir. After all, we are a highly trained and accommodating staff here at the

Hotel. In fact, you could almost say, we are programmed to receive all guests. So of course, you can check out anytime you want."

"Yeah - great, fine." I growled back, adding, "Asshole!" under my breath.

But as the door swung shut behind me and I headed out into the first pink light of cool desert dawn I thought I heard him call softly after me... "But you can never leave."

"Yeah?" I muttered stomping across the cracked asphalt of the parking lot. "Just watch me."

I threw my bag in the back seat, threw the car into gear and as I watched the structure fade in my review mirror I took a deep breath and said to the rising sun, "Never going back again."

***

The tinny blast of an air horn hit me like a physical blow. My nodding head jerked upright and I got my first hint that I wasn't going to make LA tonight. Out of the inky black of the two-lane desert highway a speeding semi inexplicably appeared in my lane....

Ric Wasley

Ric has a 40-year professional career history in advertising, publishing and marketing in Boston, New York and San Francisco. He has degrees in history and psychology and has been trained in debating, public speaking and stage acting. A large part of his 40-year career was spent in numerous professional and business settings as a presenter and featured speaker at seminars and professional meetings.

Ric has been a visiting professor at Worcester Polytech Institute. He also teaches a popular course on marketing for authors at prominent venues such as the venerable "Cape Cod Writers Conference". Ric is a published author of a Mystery Series and multiple other novels. You can visit Ric at his Website

The Ghost of Camp Wattapoopeeze

Janet Post

"I don't wanna go to camp, Mom. Please," I begged. "Lemme stay with Doug and his dad. They said I could."

Mom was driving the minivan and Ramon sat in the passenger seat. Ramon, pronounced Ra-moan, was Mom's new boyfriend. She'd met him in an online dating site. Two dates later, he'd moved in. Now they were off to a romantic cruise to Alaska for two weeks and I had to go to Camp Wattapoopeeze. Seriously, that was its name.

"I don't trust Doug's father," Mom said. "I think he's on the pot."

"It's legal, Mom. We live in Washington state."

"I don't care if it's legal. It makes him irresponsible. I mean, what's he do for a living? I've never gotten a clear picture."

"He, uh, I think he drives a delivery van."

"Then he won't be home with you two. You'll run wild. Nope, camp will do you good. You need to get out."

"No I don't. You know I hate dirt, bugs, snakes, grass, fresh air. It's all bad. And where am I going to poo? You know I have a strict pooping schedule. If I don't go by oh eight-thirty hours, I won't go all day. I always thought In military time. My real dad, not Ra-moan, had been in the Marine Corps. You know I'll get constipated, and you know how bad that is for my colon."

Ramon leaned around his seat to stare at me. "Eugene, you are worrying too much about your toilet issues. Enjoy your time at camp. Why any young man in my country would be thrilled to have the opportunity to go to such a wonderful summer camp. They have swimming, hiking, kayaking. Enjoy yourself."

Mom kind of understood. "Stop worrying, Gene. I'm sure they have WiFi."

Camp Wattapoopeeze was in Granite Falls. We lived in Everett, so not that long of a drive. Personally, I would have been happy if it lasted a lot longer. Before I had time to think, me and my backpack filled with clothes and my laptop had been deposited in the Welcome Center. The Camp Director, a sweating, overweight man with slicked-down black hair and dead eyes named Chester Weezil, smiled and shook hands with Mom and Ramon. "Don't worry," Weezil told my mom as he put his arm around my shoulders. Touching is something I don't do. I ducked and moved to stand behind Mom.

She pushed me forward. "Sorry Director Weezil, Eugene doesn't like to be touched. He has a little OCD."

Weezil laughed, a big guffaw, loud braying laugh that made my skin crawl. And while he laughed, he checked me out and his eyes didn't smile. But Mom and Ramon had a cruise to catch. So, Mom kissed me on the cheek and left me there with gross blubber-butt Chester Weezil.

The minute Mom and Ramon tooled out of the parking lot, Director Weezil's smile vanished. He pushed me. "This way. I have the perfect cabin for you."

He shoved me out the door in front of him, flagged a counselor. "Jack, take Eugene to Pinecone Cabin. I'm sure he'll be happy there."

The counselor stopped. "Really? Pinecone? You've already got three other boys there. Why not Grizzly or Mountain Lion? Grizzly only has two?"

"Mountain Lion is full, and this young man will fit in with the boys of Pinecone. Are you questioning my skills as Camp Director, Jack?"

Jack shook his head. He was tall, a jock, blond with a chiseled face and a dimple in his chin. "No, Director Weezil. I would never."

Weezil dusted his hands as though ridding himself of something dirty. "Good."

"Come on Camper," Jack said. "Don't worry about Weezil. He stays in the Welcome Center most of the time watching TV. It's the only TV we have."

"No WiFi?"

Jack laughed. "Here? Nope. If you have a cellphone, you might get service out here, but I doubt it."

He led me down a rustic trail winding through tall firs. It smelled good, like a hundred pine-scented air fresheners. We passed several log cabins. Each had a front porch with boys lounging around looking bored. I saw one staring at his phone with tears running down his face. Life without WiFi, was it worth living? On the front of each porch a plaque hung with a symbol. We passed one with a bear, must be Grizzly, one with a mountain lion, one with a big deer with huge antlers. I looked at Jack and lifted an eyebrow. I could do that because I had Bell's Palsy when I was ten and it paralyzed half my face. When the feeling came back, I could wiggle each eyebrow independently.

"Elk," Jack said correctly deciphering my unspoken question.

We finally got to Pinecone. The plaque out front had a pinecone carved into it. However, the artist must have been tired or bored because the pinecone looked more like a pile of poop. Three kids sat on the porch benches. One was kind of big, as in fat. One was a tall, skinny black kid and the last kid, half hidden behind the large kid, looked kind of Indian as in India Indian, not Tillamook Indian. "This is where you'll be camping, Camper," Jack said heartily. "Let's find your bunk."

He leaped up the steps and I dragged behind, my backpack weighing me down. I had to wait a second for my eyes to adjust to the dark interior. Jack stood next to a set of bunk beds. "You get the bottom. Rolly already claimed the top."

"Fine." I tossed my pack onto the bunk. "Where's the bathroom?" For a kid with severe OCD, which would be me, the bathroom was of premier importance.

Jack pointed to the rear of the cabin. "There's a door. You go down the path through the trees and the bath house is back there a ways. I don't advise you to spend much time in it."

I was instantly alerted. Danger, danger. My inner alarms were clanging. "Why not?"

"It's nothing. Just camp rumors and a strange legend. Forget I said anything. Spend all the time in the bath house you want."

Jack patted me on the back, and I tried not to cringe. Jack was not Director Weezil. "Come out on the porch and meet your cabinmates."

Before I followed him, I made sure my pack was lined up in the middle of my bunk. If it had been crooked, I would have found no peace until I straightened it. Satisfied, I followed him out. I didn't really want to meet my cabinmates, I mean I didn't even want to be here, but I know when to give in.

"Fellows," Jack said in his hearty councilor voice. "Meet, uh, meet." He bent low. "What's your name again? Lots of new kids. I forget."

"It's Eugene McAllen."

"Right. Guys, this is Eugene. Eugene, meet Rolland, we call him Rolly, Arthur, and Keon."

"Hey," they said listlessly.

Jack left then and there I was, alone with my cabinmates. I got right to my problem. "What's wrong with the bathrooms? Jack," I shuddered, "said not to linger in them."

The three boys immediately animated. "Dude," the chunky one called Rolly said. "It's haunted."

"Two councilors and a camper croaked in there," Keon said. "I ain't crapping til I get home."

"It is most assuredly so," Arthur said. "I heard this myself from one of the other counselors. Counselor Rajesh, told me the story."

I could feel my throat closing. In a minute, I was going to have a full-on anxiety attack of major proportions. If I couldn't go to the bathroom, I would back up like a plugged sewer line and explode. I knew this would happen. I'd tried to tell Mom not to bring me here. This was even worse than I'd imagined. "Have any of you been in it?" I managed to ask.

"I been peeing in the damn woods," Keon said. "Been here since this morning. Ain't had the chance to you know, have to use it."

"Anybody else?"

Rolly and Arthur shook their heads. "We should go check it out," I finally said. "I mean, it could be BS. Just a story to scare us made up by older boys, bullies. That stuff happens all the time."

Keon nodded. "Right. I get that shit at school. Sucks."

"You'll go with me?"

"Sure," Keon said.

Rolly piped up. "I, uh, sometimes, uh, get stomach problems, so, I, uh, have to use the bathroom a lot. I'll go."

Arthur shrugged. "if you are all going to check out the facilities, I will assuredly accompany you."

So, we left the safety of the porch, walked around the cabin, and found the path to the bath house. That's where we stopped. The path led into dark woods dripping with vines. There was no light at all. It was like night in there. The path itself was narrow. Bushes stuck out into it. Brambles had overgrown the beginning. "I can't wait here. I have to go," I said.

"Looks pretty freaky to me," Rolly said. "But sooner or later, we're gonna have to follow the path. Might as well go together. Right?"

Keon shook his head making his dread locks bob. "I don't like the dark, bugs or snakes, and I'm betting all of them things be in there."

I took a deep breath, pushed the blackberry bushes rampant in Washington aside, and stepped onto the *path.* The brambles grabbed at my jeans and my T-shirt. I tore them off, determined to find the bath house. I had to see it. No matter how terrified I was, I had to do this. I stopped and looked behind me. Keon was so close I could see the blackheads on his light-brown nose. "Dude, you need to wash your face better."

"I will," he snapped back. "Just as soon as I get my black ass home."

I shrugged. "Not really black, you know. More like light brown."

"Whatever."

Rolly was snugged up behind Keon who swatted at him. "Do not rub your belly on me."

"Sorry." Rolly backed up an inch.

"You gonna move, or stand there staring at Rolly all day?"

I laughed. "Moving right now." I pushed through more bushes and pretty soon we were in pitch darkness. The sun hadn't penetrated this forest in years. The ground was bare of vegetation and covered with a layer of needles under the thick firs. When we got close to the bath house, I smelled it. Sewage and algae and wet toilet paper smell filled the air. Then I saw the building. It was concrete block and covered with green moss on one side. Remembering long ago Boy Scout days, I figured it for the north side. The bath house had two green, slime-covered windows. The door was, of course, on the other side.

"What's that smell?" Keon asked. "Smell like doo doo."

Rolly nodded which caused his chubby cheeks to jiggle. Arthur stuck his head around Rolly. "I have smelled this odor before on the streets of Mumbai. It is most unpleasant."

"Can't stop now," I said. "We're almost there."

We walked around the building following the well-worn path. There was a door. It was green, too, just painted green. I grabbed the handle. "I'm going in."

There was no electric light inside, just a big skylight. It let in enough light to see I never wanted to be here, and I certainly didn't want to poop in here. The smell outside was nothing compared to the smell inside. The stench inside of the bath house had a rotten meat odor added to the sewage smell. A truly gross blend.

"Well, since I'm here," Keon said. "I'm checking out the facilities."

The bath house had three toilet stalls on the right with no doors. Seriously, how did they expect adolescent boys to poop in a stall with no door? On the left was a huge open shower with three shower heads. A bank of three sinks sat across from the open shower. All of the smell seemed to be coming from the toilet side. Keon stuck his head into stall number-two and the toilet exploded.

I screamed. Rolly screamed and Arthur covered his mouth. You heard that right. The toilet effluent, nice word for crap, pee and water blended into a malodorous stew, spewed out of the toilet. If I hadn't been standing there and seen it with my own eyes, I wouldn't have believed it. Keon was doused. He froze. Pieces of stringy, wet, toilet paper clung to his dreadlocks and his face and clothes. He shrieked. "Doo doo, I'm covered in doo doo."

"Come on," I urged him terrified of touching any part of his poop-covered body. I turned to Rolly, whose face was white as a sheet. "Turn on the showers. We gotta get Keon washed off quickly."

Arthur rushed to do this while I kept urging Keon to head to the shower. "Come on before you get some awful disease. Hurry."

Shuddering and shaking, Keon walking like a zombie, headed for the gushing shower. He got under just as Rolly began screaming and pointing. "Look. Oh no," Rolly yelled as he backed rapidly for the sinks.

"What now?" I looked in the direction he was pointing, and I screamed. A black demon had risen out of the same toilet that spewed filth onto Keon, stall number-two. It had red eyes and fire shooting out of its wide-open mouth. Its arms were outstretched. "Come to me," it moaned. "Come to me."

We all screamed again, and the bath house door burst open. A girl counselor followed by Jack burst into the bath house. "What's going on?" the girl yelled over the noise of our screams.

We were all backing rapidly toward Keon and the showers. Steam rose from the floods of hot water. The mirrors over the sinks were fogged. "Over there," I stuttered. "Over there."

The girl slapped her hands on her hips. She wore khaki shorts and a camp-counselor T-shirt. "This is stupid," she said and walked toward the toilets.

"No, Karen, don't." Jack lunged for her in an effort to save her as she headed for toilet number-two, but it was too late. The demon pulled her into his embrace. "Come to me," it moaned again. "Come."

Karen's wails rose from inside the demon as it took its prize and disappeared into the toilet. Karen was gone.

For a moment, we all stood frozen with horror. Not only had the demon taken Karen, but he'd taken her into the toilet which I was pretty sure led to some kind of septic system beneath the building. Turned out I was right. The floor groaned and creaked and rose into a hump. Tiles cracked. Smoke mixed with the steam and mad laughter issued from below.

That was it for me. I ran out of the bath house screaming bloody murder closely followed by my cabinmates and Jack. We pounded down the path, hit the porch steps, and rocketed into the cabin closely followed by Jack. I climbed onto my bunk and hugged my backpack. My only connection to home and safety. Jack stood in the middle of the cabin shaking like a leaf and sobbing. "Karen, what happened to you?"

Rolly climbed into the bunk over my head, rolled onto the mattress and immediately fell through landing on me and squashing me flat on my back. We lay like that for a few seconds separated only by the pack. Rolly groaned. I groaned. And he climbed off me. I sat up. "Can this get any worse?"

"We must report this terrible event to Director Weezil immediately," Arthur said. "This is most distressing. I will call my parents. They will come and get me." He took a cellphone out of his leather backpack and turned it on. "No," he gasped. "There are no bars. Not one."

Jack seemed to finally be coming around. "No service," he said in a tiny voice far from the hearty camp-counselor one he'd used before.

"Arthur is right. We need to tell Director Weezil," I said.

"Asshole won't believe us, no how, no way," Keon finally spoke. His voice shook. He was shivering with cold. "He's probably in on it."

Jack seemed to be recovering. He pushed Keon. "Go change into dry clothes." He sniffed. "And throw those away. What happened to you?"

"Before the damn toilet demon straight from freaking hell came out of the toilet, it exploded all over me."

"That would explain the smell," Jack said.

"Has this ever happened before?" I asked. My brain had finally started working.

Jack rolled his neck and stared at the ceiling. "Possibly. There have been some rumors about Pinecone's bath house."

"And you did nothing about it?" Arthur, who still clutched his useless I-Phone in his hand, asked.

"Director Weezil said it was all just kids not wanting to be at camp. Happens all the time."

"Apparently, the rumors were not rumors at all, but the truth," Arthur said.

"Let's go talk to Weezil," I said. "He's gotta do something now. That demon ate a counselor. I mean, her folks are gonna be pissed."

"We're all foster kids," Jack said. "Weezil hires foster kids as counselors. No one cares about any of us."

"That sounds very ominous," Arthur said. "Almost as though Weezil knows. I wonder if any more counselors or kids have disappeared."

Keon went and changed his clothes and we all trouped up to the Welcome Center. Weezil was in there watching TV. "Director," Jack started. "Uh, there's been an incident in the Pinecone bath house, sir."

Weezil jumped off the couch and turned on Jack. "I don't want to hear any rumors about the Pinecone bath house. How many times have I told you kids, it's all garbage, not true, made up?"

"Uh, sir," Jack went on bravely facing Weezil's bluster. "I saw a demon come out of toilet number-two and eat Karen Lentiger. She's gone, Director, sucked into the septic system."

Weezil abruptly changed his tone. He put a pudgy arm around Jack's waist. "It's time for dinner. I'll make some calls and have this looked into. Don't worry about Karen. I'm sure this is all a mistake."

"Ain't no freaking mistake," Keon snapped. "I got covered with doo doo. White girl got eaten by a black demon breathing fire with red eyes. We all saw it."

"Probably sewer gas," Weezil said. "It builds up in the septic tank. You kids were breathing it. Probably hallucinating." He urged us all out the Welcome Center door and toward a large building on top of the hill.

"Didn't hallucinate no doo doo," Keon muttered. "It was on me. I smelled it. I had toilet paper hanging from my hair."

We all went up to the dining hall to eat. I wasn't hungry. I didn't think I'd ever be hungry again. When I closed my eyes, all I saw was Karen being eaten by the demon. But the smells coming from the kitchen were inviting. "What's cooking?" I asked Jack.

"Food," he said in a quiet voice. Then he patted me on the back and I let him. I mean sometimes even I needed human contact. "Sorry, little bro, I keep thinking about Karen. She's not the first counselor to disappear. Weezil always says they either ran away or got picked up and went home. Well, I saw what happened to Karen and now I'm scared."

"We all saw. Weezil can't say she went home."

"Bet he tries to."

"Then we'll have to get rid of whatever is under the bath house ourselves. When the adults won't take care of the problems, then the kids have to."

Jack nodded and patted me on the back again. "Got that right, little bro. Hey, smells like Miss Letisha's famous meatloaf."

"Who is Miss Letisha?"

"Our cook. She's Haitian. I heard she practices a little voodoo in her cabin, but no one has ever been in there to see. She's an excellent cook. Get ready for a treat."

"I don't eat meat," I said.

Jack laughed. "Don't worry. There ain't no meat in her meatloaf. Weezil's too cheap to buy any." He looked thoughtful. "We do get a lot of chicken and hotdogs, but Miss Letisha makes it all taste great."

We followed Jack into the dining hall. The food did smell good. Keon was right behind Jack. When he spotted the big black cook serving the food, he smiled and ran forward. "Miss Letisha," he stuck out his hand and she reached over the serving line to shake his. "I didn't know you worked here."

"Only summers," she said. "I can't very well work at school, can I?"

"Miss Letisha is head of our cafeteria at Cascade High," he told me and Jack because we were standing closest. "Her food is always wonderful." He turned back to Miss Letisha. "Toilets in Pinecone bath house just exploded on me," he whispered to the cook. "Counselor got sucked in by a bad demon come right out of the damn toilet."

Miss Letisha rapidly scanned right and left. I think she was looking for Weezil. She held her finger to her mouth. "Shhh, can't talk about that stuff here in the dining hall. Come to my cabin after I get done."

Keon nodded. "Okay. Can we all come?" He indicated us with a wave of his hand.

She rolled her eyes. "If they have to."

"We all saw it, Miss Letisha. I got the doo doo on me, but they was there when the demon ate the counselor."

"Hush now. We'll talk later." Keon picked up a plate and Miss Letisha filled it with a big smile. "You boys must be hungry. Growing boys need their dinner."

We took filled plates back to the long dining tables and sat down. I toyed with the meatloaf. It smelled good, but I just couldn't. Keon pointed at the greens sitting next to a heap of mashed potatoes. "Don't eat the greens. Got pork in them. Heard you don't eat meat," he added.

"Thanks," I said. "But it's too late. I ate all of mine. I don't eat meat because I can't condone the killing of animals for food and raising large herds of cows and pigs increase greenhouse gasses. I'm basically an environmentalist. The vegetarian thing comes out of that."

"A what?"

"I want to save the planet. Global warming and all that."

Rolly looked up from his plate. "This meatloaf is terrific. You gonna eat yours?"

I pushed my plate toward him. "No, go ahead."

"He can have mine, too," Arthur said. "I don't trust it. It has a very odd odor."

"I don't know how you can smell anything," I said. "After the toilet exploded, I been smelling nothing but poop."

After we ate, we had free time, so we walked down to the lake and watched the sun set. "I'm afraid to go back to our cabin," Rolly said. "What if that thing comes out of the johns at night and grabs us."

Arthur nodded. "It will be very difficult to sleep."

"Maybe Miss Letisha can help us," Keon said. "She's a voodoo priestess back in Everett. Everybody knows her. What we need is a charm. Some powerful magic to protect us."

"I still can't believe I saw an actual demon," I said. "And it came out of the damn toilets."

We wandered back up the path toward the cabins reserved for counselors and camp employees. One of them had a red light blinking inside and candles flickering behind gauzy curtains. "That must be hers," Keon said.

We knocked and Miss Letisha opened the door. "Come on in. Hurry," she said. "Don't want old Weezil seeing you boys coming in here."

The interior of Miss Letisha's cabin was lit with a bank of black candles sitting in front of an altar decorated with beads, two skulls, a statue of a skeleton wearing a black suit, a top hat, and smoking a cigar, and at the top, a statue of the Virgin Mary. The room smelled of strange herbs and incense. Glass jars sat in a semicircle at the base of the altar. They were all empty with no lids. I looked around with interest. This was some weird shit.

We sat on cushions arranged on the floor beside Miss Letisha's bed. She sat on the bed and listened while Keon poured out the story of the exploding toilet and the demon. When he was finished, Miss Letisha sat back and pulled at her chin. "This ain't the first time we lost a counselor, no sir," she said. "Weezil always says they went back to the city, ran away, their foster parents picked them up, or some other story."

"How many have gone missing?" I asked.

"So far, four."

"Have any kids been eaten?" Rolly asked.

"We lost one last year. It caused a lot of trouble for Weezil, but that kid actually did go home. Since that one no more kids have disappeared, I'm gonna have to say Weezil is in league with the devil."

"He is a most disturbing individual," Arthur said. "I felt it from the first."

"He a bad man," Keon said. "Bad. What we gonna do, Miss Letisha? How can we kill the demon? Can't leave it in the bath house to eat counselors whenever it wants just because they're foster kids."

Miss Letisha patted Keon's head. "Yep, we're gonna have to get rid of it. Let me think about the best way to do that. In the meantime, stay out of the bath house."

"What if we have to go?" Rolly said. "I mean, I can't hold it forever. I'm gonna have to go."

Miss Letisha pulled out a map of the camp. "Use Mountain Lion's bath house. It's not that far away. You should be safe there. All the counselors were taken in the Pinecone bath house."

"Weezil put us in Pinecone cause he don't care about us," I said. "He knows what's in that bath house and he just doesn't give a shit."

Miss Letisha patted Keon on the back. "You boys better run on to the campfire sing. Weezil won't be happy if you don't show up."

"Campfire sing?" I said. "Seriously? A counselor just got scarfed by a demon and we have to go sing around a campfire like we don't know?"

"It's best to follow Director Weezil's rules," Miss Letisha said. "He can make it very hard on you boys if he doesn't like you."

"What would he do?" Rolly asked. "I mean, what could be worse than having to poop on top of a demon?"

"Well," Miss Letisha said slowly, "how would you like to have to clean *all* the bath houses with a toothbrush?"

"No!" I gasped. "That would probably kill me."

"A little OCD?" Miss Letisha asked.

"No, a lot OCD, and the germs." I shuddered. "It's not to be thought of."

"Well if he didn't make you clean toilets, he could send you on a five-mile hike with Mountain Lion," Miss Letisha said. "What do you think your chances of surviving that would be?"

"We're going to the campfire sing, okay," Rolly said. He turned to me. "If I had to hike five miles anywhere, I'd die, but with those animals? Did you see them?"

I nodded. "They're all super jocks. They'd kill us and trample our dead bodies into the mud beneath their boots."

So we followed Miss Letisha's map and headed for the campfire sing. The entire camp was sitting around a roaring fire in the middle of a cleared circle. Logs had been placed for us to sit on. We found an empty spot and plopped down. I glanced over at the group next to us. Mountain Lion for sure. The biggest kid had to be a center for some Seattle football team. If he was shorter than six-five and weighed less than three-fifty, I'd be stunned. His three partners were all no-neck, jocks. The leader appeared to be tall, blond and fit. He turned to stare at us. I cringed. Keon gave him stink eye and he shot us back the two finger, I-see-you gesture.

On our other side was an equally buff group, only less jocky more basketball player-like. Tall and lanky with two black kids. We all wore khaki shorts and Camp Wattapoopeeze T-shirts. Director Weezil stood near the fire with a big woman who wore her hair pulled into two braids. She appeared to be about forty and had legs coming out of her khaki shorts that looked like tree trunks, each one encased in high socks and sturdy hiking boots.

"That's Miss Fishguard," Keon said. "She's head camp counselor. You need something, you gotta ask her for it."

"Need what?"

He shrugged. "I don't know. Toothpaste, Band-Aid, bug-spray."

A mosquito buzzed my neck. "I could use some bug-spray right now."

"There is no way I'm asking her for anything," Arthur said.

Miss Fishguard blew into a little tuning device and sang a couple of notes in a super-deep baritone. She led us into a couple of camp songs while I slapped mosquitoes and squirmed. "How long does this last?"

"I like this song," Keon said as he wailed away on Bob Marley's Redemption Song. The next one was Home on the Range which all of us knew and none would sing. This was followed by Margaritaville. We got into that one and I was just starting to enjoy myself and relax when Rolly moaned. "I have to go."

"Go where?" Arthur asked.

"To the toilet, you know, I have to go. I ate too much meatloaf."

I looked at Keon and Arthur. They looked at me. We felt obliged to go with him. "Not going to Pinecone's bath house," Keon said. "Miss Letisha said use Mountain Lion's."

I didn't see Weezil. When I glanced around hunting for him, I saw him behind us. "Let's get out of here," I said. So we slipped out of the campfire sing and followed Miss Letisha's map to the Mountain Lion bath house. While Rolly rushed into one of the stalls, these had doors, I decided it might be a good time to use the facilities. I hadn't eaten meatloaf, but the greens were churning in my stomach. I burped, grabbed some paper towels, and carefully covered the seat before I sat down. I was just getting finished and rolling a nice wad of Mountain Lion super-thick toilet paper in my hand, when Rolly screamed.

"Please don't hurt me," Arthur wailed. "My father needs me to work in the store." I heard a bump and crying, so I pulled my pants up and climbed on the toilet to look over the top of the stall. "What you doing in our bath house, turds?" The gigantic Mountain Lion hovered over Rolly whose pants were around his ankles, tighty-whities pulled up, thank goodness.

Keon must be stupid brave or maybe just stupid because he poked the big kid in the chest. "Leave Rolly alone. We can't use our bath house, there's a demon in it. Miss Letisha said it'd be okay to use yours."

The big kid was pulling his size sixteen back to kick poor Rolly when we heard the noise. It came from stall number-two. A deep rumbling. The big kid hesitated. Super-jock with the pretty blond hair went to look and stuck his head into the stall just as it exploded. He was right next to me. I could see the whole thing over the top of the stall. When the demon rose out of the toilet, I jumped down. "Run!" I screamed.

"Poop!" Super-jock yelled. "I'm covered with the Pinecone's shit."

"Come to me," the demon moaned. "Come to me."

"Don't look at it." I said to the jock as I grabbed a corner of his T-shirt and tugged. "Whatever you do, don't look at it." I turned searching for help. Keon stood in the middle of the shower area, his coffee-colored face gray. "Keon help me. He's covered in shit. I can't touch this. I'll die."

Keon edged over. "Come on, football hero, time to run." Keon found a clean spot on the guy's shirt and shoved him toward the door. All four of the jocks were inside the bath house. We took off in a group, struggled through the door, and exploded into the chill night air.

Once outside, the horrible sounds of the demon calling ended. The four jocks from Mountain Lion stared at us. "What is going on?" Turd-covered jock demanded.

"What's your name?" Keon asked.

"Todd," he answered as he wiped a clinging piece of toilet paper off his forehead. "What the hell was that?"

"Demon," I said. "I thought it was only in the system under Pinecone. I guess it moved."

"You really must get the effluent off of you as soon as possible," Arthur said to Todd. "It contains bacteria that could make you quite ill."

"Come on," I said. "If the demon's over here, Pinecone's bath house should be okay to use."

Todd and the rest of us followed Keon to Pinecone's bath house. Todd showered while we stood outside and discussed. "How did the demon know we were going to Mountain Lion's bath house?" I asked Keon. "The only person who knew was Miss Letisha. She told us to go there. She's into voodoo. Did she call up this demon?"

"No way," Keon said. "Can't be her. I told you she works in the cafeteria in my school."

"Uh, I saw Director Weezil standing behind us at the sing," Rolly said. "I was talking about using the facilities in Mountain Lion."

"I saw him there, too," I added.

The handsome jock with the blond hair's name was Sage. The two other football players were Gary and Amos. Amos was black and Gary was the tallest of all of them. He had red hair and freckles and ears that stuck out. Todd came out of the shower in time to hear us talking about Weezil and Miss Letisha.

"So, I'm thinking, it has to be Weezil or Miss Letisha," Arthur said. "It seems obvious to point our fingers at her. She's into voodoo."

"Could be Weezil and her together," I said. "How can we trust anyone here? The whole camp could be in on this."

"Nah, ain't the whole camp," Todd said. "I know almost everyone here cause I'm like popular and most of the counselors like me cause I'm so good at sports."

"True that," Gary said in the deepest voice I've ever heard on a kid.

"Well it ain't Miss Letisha," Keon snarled. "I done told all of you, she works at my school and she's a very nice lady."

"That the cafeteria lady?" Todd asked.

I nodded. "We went to her cabin. She's into voodoo. Got an altar with skulls and shit."

"If she ain't the problem, then we need to ask for her help. If it can go to any of the bath houses more people will die," Rolly said. "And I gots to use it again." He burped, farted and ran for the door of the bath house leaving a cloud of green gas behind. "Holy shit that stinks," Amos said. "Need to sew blubber-butt's ass up."

"Don't call him bad names," Arthur said. "Just because he's a little heavy, does not make him the object of name-calling."

Todd patted Arthur on the shoulder. "Right, little bro. We're all in this together." He turned to his buddy Amos. "No more calling these guys any names. We have to stick together or someone's going to die."

"Counselors have already died," I said. "One got eaten by the demon earlier. No one cares cause they're foster kids. Weezil only hires foster kids. I'm thinking this is all him. He's the one who hires throw away teens as counselors."

"How many counselors has the demon eaten?" Gary asked in that crazy deep voice.

"Jack say four," Keon said. "So far just counselors cause Weezil don't like the fuss when campers get eaten."

"We need to go talk to this Miss Letisha," Sage said. "She seems to be the knowledgeable authority here."

Rolly emerged from the bath house fanning the air behind him. "Don't nobody go in there for at least thirty maybe forty minutes."

We climbed back up the hill. There were now eight of us. It felt so much better having the Mountain Lions with us. They were big football players. It was like we'd hired protection. The lights were out in Miss Letisha's cabin. We stopped and milled around unsure of what to do. "It's pretty late," Keon said. "She the cook. Gotta get up early and make breakfast. Maybe we should wait on this until tomorrow. I mean demon already ate one counselor. Maybe it full for now."

Todd pushed through us and banged on the door. "I just got covered in shit. We need some answers now."

Miss Letisha answered the door in a voluminous white nightgown. Her head was covered in a cap. I assumed curlers were in her hair or some kind of product. "What's on her head?" Rolly whispered to Keon.

Keon stared down at him. "Don't ever ask no black woman what's on her head. Seriously, you could die."

"Why you wakin' me up?" Miss Letisha demanded. "I gotta get up at six."

"The demon moved into Mountain Lion's bath house," Keon said. "We gotta do something. We're scared to go to bed."

"It moved?" Miss Letisha said. "That bad, very bad. If it can move around under the bath houses, it could eat a child. Or maybe it's grown or split into two." She looked us all over. "Aren't you Mountain Lions?" she asked the jocks.

"Yeah, we saw the demon in our bath house, Miss Letisha. You gotta help us."

"This is bad," she said. "Something is going on this year. Something different. Come on in."

All of us crowded into her small cabin while she lit black candles on her altar. The place smelled weird. Musky incense, a coppery smell, and there was something rotten under the house or close by.

She offered rum and a cigar to the weird skeleton statue on her altar. It wore a top hat. Then she lit a candle in front of the Virgin Mary statue. "I need to sacrifice a chicken," she said. "Papa Legba and Ghede need blood and fresh meat."

"I'll get something," Todd said and ran out of the cabin. He returned shortly carrying a plastic bag. He opened it and handed Miss Letisha an entire raw chicken. "Best we have. I know we have a chicken house at Wattapoopeeze, but I ain't watching no chickens die."

Miss Letisha took the chicken and laid it in a dish on the altar. Then she took a sharp knife and cut the palm of her hand letting the blood drip onto the chicken. The candles flickered. Miss Letisha's eyes rolled back in her head. She started speaking in a weird language. We backed to the walls as she fell onto her back and started kicking and babbling in front of the altar. I have never been so terrified. Well maybe when the demon came out of the toilet.

Someone pounded on the door of the cabin. "Open up, Letisha." It was Director Weezil. "Have you got campers in there. You know that's against the rules."

The candles suddenly went out. We stood pressed against the cabin walls in the dark, too freaked out to say a word or move. Miss Letisha kept mumbling in some foreign language and drumming her heels on the floor. The candles suddenly relit themselves. Miss Letisha jumped to her feet. The chicken was gone.

Weezil pounded on the door again. "Something going on in there Letisha. Open this door."

"Wait a minute," she said. "You done woke me up out of a nice dream."

"Bull puckey. You got kids in there."

Miss Letisha whispered into my ear. "Bathroom window."

The eight of us squished into her tiny bathroom. Todd opened the window and we climbed out. I heard Miss Letisha open her door. "This my cabin, Director," she snapped. "I expect some privacy."

I decided to stay inside the bathroom. Just me and Keon were left. We'd had to help Rolly through the window. Todd and Amos had pulled, and we'd pushed. We heard Miss Letisha slam the door. She ripped open the bathroom door. "You two, come here."

She held a bag out to us. "Take this powder and sprinkle it into the toilets the demon using," she said. "It's a powerful spell and should solve the problem."

The bag was made of black silky cloth. I took it because Keon wasn't touching it. We left her cabin after checking for Weezil and met up with the rest of our group on the path back to our cabins. I held up the bag. "We have to drop the powder inside of this bag into the toilets. Miss Letisha says it's a powerful spell and should get rid of the demon."

"I ain't going anywhere near the bath houses. Neither one of them is safe," Keon said. "I already been covered in doo doo. Once is enough."

"We could wait until morning," I said. "Do it in daylight."

"I might have to go again," Rolly moaned. "Meatloaf."

Todd and Amos stepped up. "Give the bag to us. "We'll go with Rolly."

Jack suddenly appeared. "You guys going to the bath house?"

"Where did you come from?" I asked.

"I, uh, I was doing the last bed check and your cabins are empty, so I came looking for you."

"Something weird about Jack," Keon whispered into my ear. "Do he look right to you?"

I flicked the beam from my flashlight on Jack's face. His eyes were red. "Jack's possessed!" I screamed.

Suddenly whatever had been pretending to be Jack blew up into the gigantic black demon. It hovered off the ground, a black shifting cloud of awfulness. "Come to me," it moaned with its arms outstretched. "Come to me."

We ran into the woods toward the bath house. "We need to deal with this now," I yelled to Todd as we ran. Todd nodded. "Yeah, put the stuff into one of the toilets. Gotta do it now."

I glanced behind. Rolly was falling back huffing and puffing. Arthur grabbed Rolly's hand and urged him to run faster. "Can't," he wheezed. Then he grabbed his butt. "Man, I have got to go."

First bath house we came to was Mountain Lion's. "I'll go with him," Todd said. "Give me the bag."

"Let me look at your eyes," I said to him. At this point, with Jack being one of the demons, I needed to be sure Todd was still Todd.

"Right," he said and bent over to stare into my eyes. His were blue. I smacked him on the shoulder. "Go do it. You're good."

He followed shuffling, huffing Rolly into the bath house. Keon stood beside me. "Should I go, too?"

"I'll go," Amos said and followed Todd into the bath house.

I shifted nervously from one foot to the other. "I can't wait any more," I said and followed Amos inside. It was as dark as a tomb in the bath house. With no electric lights, all we had were our flashlights. I shone mine around the damp, stinky room and saw Todd stepping toward the center toilet with his hand holding the bag. He turned his head to look at me and went in. It took two seconds and he was out of the stall and running. "It's bubbling," he screamed.

"What about Rolly?"

"He'll have to fend for himself. He's roosting."

"Rolly?" I called as I inched toward the first stall. "You okay?"

Rolly groaned. "I've got bubble guts." He blasted a huge fart and groaned again.

"That should teach you not to eat so much."

"Oh no," Rolly screamed. "The toilet is boiling."

I decided, even though the thought was disgusting, to help Rolly. Amos followed me, his taller body casting weird shadows across me. I was only about two feet from the stall door when it blasted open pushed by Rolly who shot through the air like a torpedo and belly flopped on the concrete floor. His pants were around his ankles with a vast expanse of his behind showing. I shielded my eyes, grabbed one arm, Amos grabbed the other, and we hoisted him up enough to drag him out of the bath house. The toilets, all three, boiled and shot sewage over the top of the stall walls hitting the metal roof. The stench was incredible.

Arthur, Todd and Keon met me and Amos at the door. They grabbed Rolly and hauled him out onto the forest floor. He lay there like a beached whale panting and chuffing, but he was alive and that was all that mattered at this point. We couldn't lose anyone. It was unthinkable.

"That was awesome," Sage said. Todd fist-bumped him.

"Think we got rid of it?" Todd asked. "I used most of the stuff in the bag." He held it up. The bag was still half full.

A rumble came from inside the bath house followed by screeching banshee noises, then the familiar moan. "Come to me. Come to me."

"No, I don't," I said. "Give me the bag."

We ran, thundering through the woods, crashing into tree branches, with thorns and brambles ripping our clothes, as we followed the narrow trail to Pinecone's bath house at a dead run. Rolly trailed behind. He'd pulled his jeans up and was limping. "Oh, my stomach hurts," he wailed.

We stopped at the Pinecone bath house. "Don't tell me you have to go again."

"I can't help it."

"Dude," Todd said. "If I were you, I'd take my chances in the woods."

"No," Rolly said. "I couldn't. There's no way I can poop in the woods."

"Then you're going to have to risk Pinecone's bath house."

"What about the Grizzly bath house?" He said.

I examined the camp map Miss Letisha had given me. "Grizzly is too far away. I think you'd be better off trying to make it to the Welcome Center. It's probably safer, too."

Amos groaned. "My stomach hurts, too."

"Did you eat the meatloaf?" I asked.

He nodded. "Two helpings."

"Shit," Todd said. "Let's get them to the Welcome Center. My guts are churning, too."

I shook my head. "You ate the meatloaf?"

He nodded and I sighed. "Well someone has to stay here and put the powder from Miss Letisha's gris gris bag into stall number two. I guess that will be me."

Todd handed me the bag. Keon and Arthur stepped beside me. "We'll go with you."

"Thanks guys," I said with real gratitude. "This could be dangerous."

"We got your back."

So Todd took Rolly and Amos, Gary and even Sage all moaning and clutching their bellies, up to the Welcome Center, while we faced the bath house from hell. "Shine your lights in there," I said.

We beamed all three of our lights on the interior of the Pinecone bath house. I was shaking so hard my light flickered. I don't think I'd ever been this scared before in my life. This is what happens when your mom starts dating on the internet. "Ready?" I asked.

"Hell no," Keon said. "I ain't never gonna be ready for this. Better not get any more doo doo on me. I'll be mad then, really mad. And anything might happen then. Let's do this."

I led seeing as how I had the bag with the charm in it, hands shaking, heart pounding so hard I was afraid I'd stroke out. I slowly entered the bath house, shined my shaking flashlight every way, saw nothing. "I think it's clear."

I inched toward stall number two, suddenly glad there were no stall doors. I could see the john just sitting there all innocent like, shiny, white, empty. I took a big pinch of the powder and Keon smacked me in the back. "Just dump it all in there."

"Good plan."

With him right behind me, I rushed into the stall, he held the light, and I dumped the contents of the bag into the water swirling in the toilet. *Why is the water swirling?* "It's gonna blow!" I screamed.

We turned to run and there was Jack standing in the door blocking our exit. "Going somewhere boys?" His red eyes glowed.

I turned the bag upside down and shook the residue into my hand, it wasn't much, just a few grains of powder and a chicken bone. I threw it in the demon's face. Jack screamed as the powder got into his eyes and the chicken bone thunked him in the head. Keon pushed me aside. "Want out," he snarled. "Want out of here."

He tackled Jack, knocked the demon down, and we trampled across his body on our way out of the bath house. Arthur was waiting. "Jack came out of nowhere," he mumbled. "I, uh, I couldn't move. He touched me and look." Arthur showed me his arm. It was covered with poop.

Jack scrambled to his feet awkwardly. There was something stiff about his movements I couldn't put my finger on. Keon did it for me. "Damn Jack look like a freaking zombie."

"Run!" Artur screamed.

We raced up the path in the pitch dark, falling, scrambling over fallen logs, clothes ripping to shreds on brambles. I tried to use my flashlight, but I was moving too fast. We popped out in the clearing containing the Welcome Center. There was the rest of our group standing at attention around a blazing fire. "It's gotta be Weezil," Keon said. "He must be behind all this."

"I don't think it's just Weezil," I said backing toward the woods. "In fact, I don't think it's Weezil at all. Look."

On the ground in front of an altar covered with black candles and the skeleton guy in the tux lay Director Weezil. Miss Letisha hovered over him holding a dead chicken. She dripped the blood from the chicken's neck across his prone body and chanted. Every time she said," Rise," the group of boys standing around Weezil chanted, "Rise."

"This is bad," Keon said. "So bad. I never woulda thought it was Miss Letisha."

Jack pushed me in the back, and I screamed. Miss Letisha glanced up and saw us. She beckoned. "Come to me," she moaned. "Come to me."

Arthur ran to the altar. Not to obey her, but to stop her. Apparently, because we had not consumed the dreaded meatloaf, she couldn't control us. I felt a compulsion to obey her, but ran after Arthur instead. He tackled Miss Letisha, shoving her on top of Director Weezil. When she fell across Weezil, he groaned, shook his head and pushed himself to his knees.

I grabbed his arm. "Run," I hissed. "Get out of here."

Arthur and I leapt to our feet. I hunted for Keon and gasped. He'd joined the group of boys, which included poor Rolly, circling the fire. "He is a believer," Arthur said. "His beliefs have trapped him."

"Not me," I snarled and raced into the darkness following Weezil.

The Director ran to his cabin and we followed. I could still hear the chanting back at the fire. A black cloud rose above the sparks and flames. I recognized it. Toilet demon.

"Get in here," Weezil commanded. Arthur and I followed Weezil into his cabin. He slammed the door and stood with his back against it panting. "That was close."

"In the name of Shiva what is going on?" Arthur demanded.

"Letisha is a voodoo priestess. How was I supposed to know? She works for the county at school. I thought she was a good hire." He began to cry. "Now she's taking control of my beloved park. I love Camp Wattapoopeeze. It's been my passion for twenty years." His sobs of anguish filled the small cabin. "When I was a boy, I came here. It was the only time in my childhood I remember having fun." He wailed. "My parents were so strict, and I was a fat kid, but here, everyone treated me like I was normal. I had freedom. I learned to canoe and build fires. I loved the singing so much." He fell onto the bed and dropped his head into his hands. "What are we going to do? What can we do? She's got the jocks now. She turned them into zombies."

I glanced at his walls. Swords of every description hung in racks on all the walls. He must have a hundred. "How do you kill a zombie?" I asked Arthur.

"Decapitation and then you destroy their brains."

"Nice, but these are fellow campers. We can't cut off their heads."

"Then we have to take out Miss Letisha and that will not be an easy task." He indicated the swords. "While killing them should be simple. Just a matter of using these swords and whoosh, slicing off their heads, Eugene is correct, we cannot kill children, even jocks are somebody's child."

"Uh," Weezil stared at me. "You're Eugene, right?"

I nodded. "We need to come up with a plan."

A loud shriek and groaning echoed through the night outside the cabin. "We better invent this plan soon," Arthur said. "Or we're going to be added to the zombie army."

"Have you got a computer?" I asked Weezil.

He pointed to a small desk with a closed laptop.

"Does it have internet?"

"I use my hot spot on my phone."

"Well boot it up. We'll Google it."

"In minutes, I was surfing the internet looking for a way to cure Letisha's zombies. I read about how she'd created them using zombie powder and I read about Ghede, the spirit that controls zombies. He wore a top hat. I knew that figure. It was on the altar in Letisha's cabin. Google said Ghede could be bribed. He was an alcoholic. So that was what the rum had been for. Then all those jars she had on the altar. They must contain the petite spirits of all the jocks and Jack. If we opened the jars and broke them, the spirits would re-inhabit the boys and they wouldn't be zombies anymore. Google also said zombies could be rendered inanimate with salt, but too much would kill them, and they were terrified of frogs.

Weezil and Arthur read over my shoulder. "We must break the jars," Arthur said.

Weezil agreed. "But how do we get rid of Letisha?"

"Gonna have to be the swords," I said and shuddered.

Armed with Samurai swords, the three of us snuck out of Weezil's cabin and moved quietly through the scrub to the back of Letisha's. I peeked into the only window. It looked empty. We could still hear the chanting coming from the bonfire area. "Let's do this," Weezil said.

Weezil took out his master key and opened Letisha's door. Black candles burned on the weird altar with the statue of Ghede. Seven jars sat on a shelf around the altar. There were four jocks, Jack, Rolly, and now Keon. That must be the seven petit souls. There was one big jar with no lid on it. "I bet that one's for me," Weezil moaned. "She's been trying to trap me for days."

"Then how could you allow kids to come here knowing she was evil?"

"I wasn't sure," he pleaded. "I thought maybe I was hallucinating. I've been taking a new blood pressure medicine."

"You knew and you allowed it," Arthur said in his most adult voice. "One of the counselors died because of you."

"And what about last year? Jack said five counselors disappeared last summer."

"I thought they'd run away," Weezil whined. "I was only trying to help them. Foster kids, you know, they have terrible home lives. I was trying to give them a chance. I just thought they ran for it." Weezil sobbed into his hands. "I really thought they ran."

"You're a bad man," Arthur said.

I turned on Arthur. "He's fixing it now, Arthur. Lighten up. He was trying to do a good thing by bringing foster kids out to the camp. Let's get these jars broken."

Weezil opened the jars and I hacked them with my sword shattering the glass. When the glass on the first one broke, we heard a terrible screech come from the bonfire area. "Hurry," Weezil cried. "She knows. Oh, please hurry."

So, we shattered the jars even the big empty one, and started to run. I turned back. "Let's burn this place."

"What?" Weezil gasped. "But it's one of my cabins."

"You want her back in business?" I snarled not believing I was speaking to an adult like this.

"No, of course not," he whimpered.

"Run you two. I'll do it."

They left the cabin and I tipped over all the candles with my sword. Hangings, offerings on the weird altar, and the rug caught on fire. In seconds, the interior of the cabin was in flames. I rushed out the door and ran right into Miss Letisha. She grabbed me and I fought her. She was so strong. I couldn't believe it. Even though I fought like my life depended on it, she got me on the ground and was choking me. I saw Jack run up right behind her. He picked up my dropped sword and lopped off her head. Thick, black blood spurted out all over me. I have never been so horrified in my life. Her head, mouth wide open, eyes bugging out of the sockets, rolled off into the woods on its own power. Jack chased it hacking at it with the sword as I tossed her twitching body off me and jumped to my feet shrieking. Jack was screaming, the jocks showed up and they screamed. Weezil and Arthur popped out of the woods and they screamed. We were all shrieking and yelling.

As the sun rose over the tops of the trees, I ran, still screaming and followed by the jocks, Arthur and Weezil, down to the lake. I plunged into the cold water ignoring the probable bacteria, parasites, and ear worms no doubt hiding in there, and washed Letisha's black blood off me. We'd all finally stopped screaming when Karen, the counselor who'd been eaten by the toilet demon, rose out of the water and walked to the shore followed by five other counselors. They looked pretty soggy and pale, but otherwise seemed okay.

Weezil fell on them. "I'm so sorry. I should have stopped her last year. I just wasn't sure it was her. I thought you'd all run away, and I didn't want to get into trouble." He hugged each one. They seemed confused and disoriented. "What happened?" Karen asked.

Weezil led us up to the Welcome Center where the counselors who'd been taken sat down. Jack and Weezil explained everything to them. They were horrified and shocked but remembered nothing.

Rolly, Keon, Arthur and I went back to our cabins and slept for a whole day and a night. Weezil hired another cook and I spent two weeks learning to build fires, swim, canoe and ride horses. It turned out to be the best summer of my life. I'll always remember it. When my mother showed up to get me, the car was empty. "Where's Ramon?" I asked as I tossed my pack into the back.

"He ran off with one of the dancers from the ship," she said.

"Aren't you upset?"

She shrugged. "Not really. He was starting to get on my nerves. How was your summer?"

I grinned. "Best summer ever. Thanks, Mom."

"She smiled as we headed back to Everett. "I knew you'd love camp."

Janet Post

Janet calls herself a military brat from Hawaii. She worked as a reporter for years before retiring to write books. Horses and dogs are her passion along with writing adventure. She now lives in Florida with her active family and a slew of pets.

Tell-Tale Publishing would like to thank you for your purchase. If you would like to read another of our anthologies, or more by some of these fine TT authors featured in the anthology, please visit our website:

www.tell-talepublishing.com